DODGER BLUE WILL FILL YOUR SOUL

Camino del Sol
A Latina and Latino Literary Series

Dodger Blue Will Fill Your Soul

BRYAN ALLEN FIERRO

THE UNIVERSITY OF
ARIZONA PRESS

TUCSON

The University of Arizona Press
www.uapress.arizona.edu

Printed in the United States of America
21   20   19   18   17   16   6   5   4   3   2   1

ISBN-13: 978-0-8165-3275-9 (paper)

Cover designed by Leigh McDonald

Publication of this book is made possible in part by the proceeds of a permanent endowment created with the assistance of a Challenge Grant from the National Endowment for the Humanities, a federal agency.

Library of Congress Cataloging-in-Publication Data
Names: Fierro, Bryan Allen, author.
Title: Dodger blue will fill your soul / Bryan Allen Fierro.
Other titles: Camino del sol.
Description: Tucson : The University of Arizona Press, 2016. | Series: Camino del sol
Identifiers: LCCN 2015046820 | ISBN 9780816532759 (pbk. : alk. paper)
Subjects: LCSH: Hispanic Americans—California—Los Angeles—Fiction. | LCGFT: Short
    stories.
Classification: LCC PS3606.I3677 A6 2016 | DDC 813/.6—dc23 LC record available at http://lccn.
    loc.gov/2015046820

for my mother and grandmother,
Rosalia and Amina Fierro

On that long westward morning, all the Mexicans
still dreamed the same dream. They dreamed of being
Mexican. There was no greater mystery.

—Luis Alberto Urrea, *The Hummingbird's Daughter*

CONTENTS

DODGER BLUE WILL FILL YOUR SOUL

PROLOGUE

Anabel Flores remembered how she first felt when she was forced to read that book about the girl who loved that guy who remembered something about his past, and how his past really messed shit up between the two, and how it was supposed to be a book about how not to fall in love when the match is less than something someone would describe as top-notch. She hated it. And when her babies cried in the middle of the night, she would read that book so as not to come fully awake. And they'd cry well past the scene where the guy says that he would be there forever. Then came the two-page kiss. Anabel called bullshit: she's heard that mess before and has the blown-out hips as proof.

Anabel worked evenings, six days a week at the Montebello Towne Center, at a store called Fashion Nova. *The pay, no mames, the pay!* She folded and unfolded slim-fit V-necks and the short-waisted cardigans the valley hueras wore to show off asses that needed no introduction. She took the garbage down the long underground mall corridors, down to the food court Dumpster, where she'd recount her job and nights to Emilio at Hot Dog on a Stick, the Montebello Towne Epicenter, where mostly young girls teased lemonade after school. They accepted Emilio because he ran with pretty boys on Saturday nights.

"This shit can't be it for me, right?" asked Anabel.

And Emilio winced as she detailed how in the middle of the night her babies cried and cried and sucked her nipples raw into a hardened nub that hinted the last-known whereabouts of a missing appendage. While Emilio nodded his head at Anabel, the book about volatile love now shimmed the right side of the washing machine in her parents' garage across town in Whittier, stabilizing the effects of uneven loads and soaking up linty water from an unreachable leak where the hose attached to the machine's back side at an angle just so, rusting wobbly sheet metal that bent inwardly and bowed outwardly with the faint sound of thunder trapped inside a box canyon.

Anabel explained that she had read the book at night in order to not come fully awake while her babies clasped her downturned breast. The woman in the book was named Lola. Lola's lover reminded Anabel of a fast car. They lived in the South—not La Puente, or El Monte, but the South-South. She couldn't name all the states that took up space there, but she did know the houses, described in the book as big and white and pillared. This was the part of the book she didn't mind so much, the part she thought that maybe if read aloud might sound arranged to music.

She asked Emilio, "Have you ever read this book?"

He looked up from the frozen packs of hot dogs, some of which were now fully thawed, some with the cornmeal split at the center from misshapen sticks. "I don't think I've read anything better, Ana, except maybe my Silver Surfer collection, 'cause you know the Silver Surfer is a clean-chromed galactic badass."

He explained to Anabel how the Silver Surfer searches the galaxies, selecting planets for the mighty Galactus to devour, so that he might feed the unfillable void and the loss that is his astro-hearted metabolism. He explained to her that the Silver Surfer only heralds space for Galactus so that he might spare his own planet in the long run, and return to his truest love, that otherworldly super-fine morena, Shalla-Bal. Emilio kicks this down to Anabel in such a way that she suspects the Silver Surfer just might be in the next room listening to it all, his chromed-out ear pressed to the unpainted drywall of the storeroom, nodding his head with some sense of relief that someone else understood, someone different from him, but just like him. This was the image in Anabel's head, and she placed her palm against the wall to feel the Silver Surfer's celestial heat.

"Galactus?" she asked Emilio, holding the shrug of her shoulders at their peak.

"A big ol' pimp. Like my brother—he's Efraín-sized, muscles drawn on muscles, fists of anvils one hundred feet high."

"Tell me," said Anabel, "does the Silver Surfer find his love after roaming those galaxies for Galactus?"

"For reals, Ana?" Emilio blew her a kiss. "Everything is a love story, mija. And they only end one way."

She pulled her hand away from the storeroom wall, embarrassed that she might've revealed the burned-out, star-sized hole in her own chest, and how she has never spent time with a book or a man cover to cover. She did think to show the South-South and the Silver Surfer the vibrant Planet Los Angeles—Monterey Park, Montebello, and Pico Rivera—and Mexican singsong between Beverly Boulevard and Atlantic Boulevard and Rosemead Boulevard and the 605.

And it went like this . . .

BETO ORDOÑEZ

Beto sat in the convent basement as he watched the space shuttle *Challenger* explode over the Atlantic Ocean and rain down million-dollar space trash. He watched the CNN live feed with his class on a black-and-white Magnavox he had helped wheel from the rectory across the playground. Thanh Nyguen and Chris Ochoa pressed their fingers to the screen, announcing solid rocket boosters *here* and fuselage *there* until seventy-three seconds into it all, when everything space-age burst into a pitchforked column of smoke and indistinguishable superplastic parts. Beto sat with his feet propped up on the desk at the back of the room. He held the remote control out in front of his body in a way that suggested he might've masterminded the whole thing from Continuation Catholic Development camp.

"Say something," he commanded, escalating ticks of volume as the telecast fell silent. "Man, oh man, did you see that? That was something else. There are special effects and then there are *special effects.*"

Sister Viramona pushed Beto's feet off the desk and took the controller. "I expect more from you."

"I'm sorry, Sister, but did you see that thing all blown apart to smithereens?"

Sister Viramona shook Beto's arm and directed him to stand with the other children who had all come together to make a circle in the prayer room, under the large crucifix that held all the space on the far wall from floor to ceiling.

"That's a giant-ass Jesus," Beto exclaimed.

Thanh Nyguen nodded.

Beto leaned back to get a look at the television. He tapped on Chris Ochoa's shoulder. "Check it. Space trash takes a long time to fall." They watched the looping footage of the shuttle breaking apart into a fireball that seemed to eat up everything inside itself before spreading outward across the sky. Beto was surprised every time the shuttle took flight, that it did the same thing over and over again, anticipating its destruction, each time with a great *whoa!* "I bet it's ten thousand degrees in that cockpit."

Some of the children whimpered softly. Giant-ass Jesus has that effect on the little ones, Beto thought. "What are you crying about?" He addressed two girls holding hands. "You didn't know no one on that rocket ship."

"That's enough, young man. When we're done here, we are gonna have a little talk."

He deeply inhaled Sister Viramona's lavender scent as she walked past to change the channel. Little bolts of blue static shot from under her polyester robe as it dragged along the carpet. "You don't smell like a nun," Beto said. "You smell like the perfume my moms used to wear when she she'd go out dancing."

"I don't wear perfume. And I don't appreciate you—"

"You wear makeup, too. I can see it right there. It's not as much as my moms—used to take her an hour sometimes to get her eyebrows kickin'." Beto clasped his hands in prayer and bowed his head. "It looks tight on you, though, Sister." Beto concentrated on the last image he had of his mother. Her hair arched high in a great wave. He had buried his face in her chest to say good-bye. The glitter from her lotion had stayed on his cheeks the entire weekend. Beto thought she resembled the caged, naked woman in the oil lamp that hung over the far end of the family couch. Hot oil droplets ran down the cage bars in a spiral, evenly spaced and lighted by a red bulb. Both had wide hips and sparkled like goddesses.

Sister Viramona wore soft hints of makeup that he had never seen on a nun. That's the reason he'd mentioned it. Beto had never seen such a pretty, young-looking nun. Her habit cupped the edge of her face and forced the flesh around her lips into a constant pucker. She was attractive, much like the kiosk makeup counter girls at the Pico Rivera Towne Center. And she was the same height as him. He noticed how their hands were the same size, hers matching evenly over the top of his as she dragged him to the prayer room. They were soft baking hands, always in oil and corn flour, and unlike the other nuns' hands, the old nuns who looked like the stocking dolls he had made for the craft fair, with their potato faces and pinto bean eyes. Their hands were callused stumps from spending so much time in the church garden pulling up crabgrass and daffodils. No, Sister Viramona was the freshest nun he had ever seen, someone he might consider inviting out for a game of bones with his boys. When the other kids Our Fathered, Beto repeated in his head, *You are the prettiest, you are the prettiest*, to Sister Viramona, and then he prayed a deep prayer that she somehow had gotten the message.

"I don't know what you're up to," Sister Viramona said.

"Space shuttle don't blow up every day, Sister," answered Beto. "I know peoples died, but peoples die."

"You scare the other kids when you talk like that. You're older, Beto. They look up to you."

"Eleven years old ain't old," Beto said. "They'll be all baptized up like me someday."

"Who used that word, *baptized*?"

Beto pointed to giant-ass Jesus across the room.

"Baptized by fire," Beto said. "Just like them." He tapped on the screen and counted down until the shuttle vaporized for the twentieth time that morning. "All burned up. Right there, see that? That box holds all the astronauts. If it falls any faster, there'll be a mile of dead fish in the ocean before it stops."

Sister Viramona shook her head.

He called out, "Torpedoes!"

Beto turned his attention to a sweep of crows outside the classroom window. Each crow dipped into the church garden, pecking at felled tomatoes like it was some kind of game. They were on the convent roof that stretched to the rectory in an L shape. They flew out from the garden and landed on the telephone wires. They cawed and pecked at the plumage that rose from their backs in blue-black mohawks. It was as if they were taunting Beto, who could do nothing about their numbers.

Beto karate-kicked the curtains and banged on the window before unplugging the television. He pushed it across the playground, past Father Lynch, who was smoking a cigar and playing kickball with some of the children, ash swirling on them like some sort of blessing. He pushed the television up the back ramp into the rectory living room, and lined up the wheels with the divots already cut into the carpet, plugged everything back into the outlets, and turned it on. This time there was no footage of the shuttle, only a picture of a woman he had seen on the news for the last few months. She was the teacher, Christa McAuliffe. Under her image it read, *First female teacher in space*. Beto looked around to comment that she never actually made it into space, but the rectory was empty.

The entire *Challenger* crew had their picture on the television. One looked like Sulu from *Star Trek*. Another, Issac from *The Love Boat*. When CNN came back to McAuliffe's picture, *planned* had been added to her title in parentheses. He felt relieved knowing NASA wouldn't be allowing Carmelites into the space program anytime soon. The newscast suggested it was possible that the crew could still be alive, that the cabin of the shuttle was made of reinforced aluminum and could handle a significant amount of g-force. Beto thought about the time he had ripped a Coke can in half on the first try, and then shut off the television.

The morning's events drove a hunger stake through Beto's stomach. "Gotta get me some eats." He remembered the altar boys telling him after Mass on Sundays how they had to stock the Christ crackers. He knew what these were. Beto grew up going to Mass with his grandparents. This was so his mom could get away for a while, take her trips to visit her cousins in Monterey Park, where she'd go dancing all night at Peppers. He'd go to Mass those weekends and be amazed every time Father Lynch reached into the chalice after the Consecration that there were enough pieces of Christ's body for everyone to get their fill, like some kind of magic trick: *Watch, it's gonna be a rabbit next*. Every time, he thought *that* Sunday would be *the* Sunday they'd run out of Christ. It never happened. The more people who came to the front, the more pieces Father held in front of his face reciting, *The body of Christ*. But it made sense now, standing in the rectory storeroom, there on the shelf in a cardboard box—Jesus, wrapped all up in yellowing wax paper like a Ritz.

He rubbed his sweaty palms against his jeans and opened the package's seam at one end. The hosts appeared like a roll of gold coins, each with a cross on one side in relief. Beto pulled a cracker out and hesitated, then put it deep into the back of his mouth, half expecting his head to explode. He felt a slow dissolve on his tongue and a wood-like taste that he surprisingly did not mind. Jesus dried Beto's mouth all up, and when the good Lord started to stick to the roof of his mouth, the blood of Christ did the trick to help pry Him out.

He couldn't wait to tell his boys. He would stand baggy on the corner and his boys would say, *You did what?* And Beto would respond, *That's right, putos.* And when they called him "crazy-ass Beto," he'd do his best to act as though the next thing didn't happen. He wouldn't mention how the scent of vanilla mixed with lavender from around the corner filled his head, or that he never expected to act like a girl the way he did after spilling a box of red wine down the front of Sister Viramona's robe. It froze the nun in place like a black-and-white snapshot. Beto sensed that the compassionate Sister was using all her divine intervention to control her response. It was as if she spoke in tongues, a hundred different responses broken up into fractured syllables that floated and fell on Beto like scorched space trash.

"Why in God's name do you do these things, Beto?"

He shrugged. "It just takes me over sometimes, Sister."

"Beto, there is so much devil in you." She dried herself with the Kleenex from her pockets that appeared equally soaked. "What do you expect from life, acting this way?"

His mom would ask him the same question when he'd get in trouble at home, usually for coming home late from Cabrillo Beach, where he'd spend the day looking for dead pelicans. He gave her the same answer he always gave his mother: "To take over the world."

"Great, we have ourselves a supervillain."

He liked the sound of that, and pumped his fists.

Sister Viramona shook her head and told Beto that he would be spending a late afternoon at the convent washing the largest Jesus in Montebello as the first act of penance before a sit-down with Father Lynch.

"I have to get cleaned up. You're coming with me. I don't want you out of my sight for too long."

Beto had already had his first *and* last confession as far as he was concerned! The confessional always smelled like incense, bacon grease, and old Mexican women. You know, that sour body odor. They were the ones who went to confession most often. He wondered what old women did to warrant going to confession once a week. Then he remembered Mrs. Mendoza. Mrs. Mendoza had taught first grade to three generations of his family. She was the oldest teacher in the school district when she retired at dinosaur. On Thursday nights, she chased Mr. Mendoza down the block with the family molcajete. Thursday night was the night he came home drunk and only spoke of pretty girls named Luba. Everyone knew this. Go ahead and ask. And after the couple attended Mass and confession on Sunday, all was forgiven. Beto watched them those Sundays as they walked out after Mass, hand in hand, laughing like the schoolchildren. Confession worked. So, as long as the confessional did not shift and fly like the Swirl-n-Whirl ride at the Santa Monica Pier, he felt okay about some small talk inside. He threw up two years in a row on the Swirl-n-Whirl. His mother had yelled at him for wasting good money on churros and hot dogs. She told him they would never come back to the pier because, after all she's done for him, including giving up a dancer's body to bring him into the world, he was becoming the kind of boy who would have to make his own way into manhood. That was a week before she died instantly in a fiery rollover on the 60, driving home from Peppers after a night of dancing with her girls, like some kind of stupid motherly lesson.

"You know, Beto, you're lucky no one is here." She walked out from the bedroom and pulled her straight black hair under a plastic band. "Because I'd get in trouble." She had on navy sweatpants and a 1972 Sacred Heart Volleyball sweatshirt. "I didn't plan on you pouring wine on me."

Beto's body felt like a firecracker, his spine the lit fuse to a head that was going to jettison at any moment. He swallowed hard. "Nuns play sports?"

"Four years varsity, actually," she said. "All-state."

Beto stepped closer. "My mom went to that school."

"I know she did, Beto. Stay here, okay, and I'll get the supplies."

The crows were back, darting from the roof again into the remains of the garden. Beto pointed out their tactics as Sister Viramona reentered the room, tracing their flight patterns overhead with his index finger pressed against the large bay window. "See how they look out for each other? It's a damn stupid thing, those crows. You missed them this morning, Sister. It was just like that movie *The Birds*. You watch. I bet Father Lynch goes crazy and machetes those birds someday. That'll be a day to remember for the parish, Sister. If they poked around in my trash, I'd do the same thing."

A half dozen more crows danced in the middle of the street.

She placed her hand on Beto's shoulder. "You know, Beto, I didn't know her."

Beto nodded and took a bottle of lemon oil and two rags made from T-shirts from the last year the Dodgers made it to the postseason, a large-headed cartoon version of Fernando Valenzuela. Again, he felt the softness of her touch.

You're the prettiest, he tried one last time.

She let go, and for the first time Beto could smell the real air in the convent, no vanilla or lavender, only the musty rot of a building with trapped moisture problems.

Sister Viramona bent at her waist to get a good look at Beto. He stiffened his body, and through the slits in his eyelids, he watched as she ran her finger between the top of her head and the plastic band, pulling her hairline tight. She squeezed his arms to undo his spell, her warm breath on his face, prying his eyes open like oysters.

"Beto, there is a time and place for everything," she told him.

These words—*time* and *place*—sounded like something he'd expect to hear from an adult.

"Time and place for what?" Beto asked.

"Taking over the world." She faced the prayer room and whispered across the back of his neck, "And falling in love."

Beto shadowboxed his image against the wall. "Man, oh man, watch out, watch out."

"The Lord won't let you off so easy." Sister Viramona lined up the cleaning supplies on the counter and walked to the back of the convent.

Beto mumbled, "I'm gonna need me a good woman, you know."

Sister Viramona did not respond.

The only thing left to do was clean giant-ass Jesus all up. He scrubbed each toe, both calf muscles, the knees, and behind each thigh. He cleaned the concave of the stomach and gently over the cut below the rib cage, looking to Jesus's face to measure His pain. Beto moved to the chest and under each arm, where he spent a considerable amount of time measuring the Savior's biceps—"Boy, you *all* kinda ripped up, Jesus"—down each arm to the nail in each palm. He used WD-40 on any part that looked metallic and moveable. He didn't miss a finger, then under the chin and behind each ear. It looked as though this was the first time Jesus had been cleaned. The water turned black. He was careful not to cut himself on the already bloodied thorns of the life-sized crown as he leaned in from the top step of the ladder.

Beto put the used rags under the sink in the kitchen. He didn't know if it was where they belonged, but it was where his mother had kept such things. Sister Viramona was in her room at the end of the hall. She hadn't told him to check with her before leaving. He could hear music coming from her far room, a popular song he knew from the radio. It called to him, and he wanted to go down to her, to let her know he was no mistake. The shadows in her room flickered and the music grew louder. The other nuns were off on retreat. Beto thought about the first time he was alone at home, back when his mother had to work two full-time jobs. The evening had been spent practicing his mother's dance moves from the club. He ate ketchup and pickle sandwiches, and turned the television volume to fifty. He ran around the house at full speed, stopping for no one.

DODGER BLUE WILL FILL
YOUR SOUL

Mariana says Steve Garvey is mas chingon and has the forearms of a dream husband. "Arms that could hold me all night long," she says to your face. She does her dance in the kitchen, the dance she did last night in the middle of the living room, a little salsa number she does during every Los Angeles Dodgers game, every time number six comes up to the plate. She does this dance to bring luck. Your nine-year-old son, Isaac, who criminally does not watch Dodger ball, dances with Mariana on the linoleum, matching his mother's steps, side to side. He dances without knowing his role as a Dodger fan.

A four-game stretch against the Houston Astros is stressful. Tonight you will watch game two of the series on the nineteen-inch TV with tinfoil and taped rabbit ears. Isaac laughs every time you try and improve the reception, mistaking poverty for ingenuity. He has seen you do this with the refrigerator, the clothes dryer, and all his RC cars.

Isaac runs in and out of the house, not paying attention to the game. When strike three is called on Bill Russell to end the first, you let Isaac know as he passes through the living room, just to keep him involved in the game. "Strike three, Isaac. You hear me?"

He finally settles down when cousins from *your* family's side arrive in the top of the third inning. They're a group of Mexicans that stumble into your two-bedroom home. They have long moustaches and teardrop tattoos leaking from the corner of their eyes. These are the cousins you never wanted to visit as a boy, back when you were the same age Isaac is now. They lived in Pico Rivera when you lived in Monterey Park. You just didn't know how to talk to them, a mother tongue plucked out like tonsils. The girls were always nice to you. They spoke magic and called you soft Mexican names reserved for lost children. The second name on all your records is pobrecito. The boys wanted to see what you were made of. They hardly said a word to you at all, and when they finally opened up, they only asked questions about the girls you've been in, and then hissed laughter at your answers. When you said you were hungry, the boys gave you salted dried plums that you hid in a paper towel inside your dead uncle's work boots that never left the back porch. The girls made you bean and cheese burritos and squeezed your cheeks as you ate. They took you into their room and let you place the needle on *Thriller*. You picked out their nail polish and never chose black. The boys stalked you in the house like a wounded gazelle. They tackled you and bent you over so your full stomach was pinched and you couldn't breathe. And now you are here in Pico and there's not much you can do anymore to avoid these situations, and even as a grown man, the air in your lungs escapes you. Your primo Hector pulls up his shirt to let Isaac trace his Our Lady of Guadalupe tattoo with an index finger. Isaac starts on the right side of her unenthusiastic look that says she has given up ever coming off Hector's flaco chest, and works his way around. This is the moment Hector announces that he is taking Isaac to get his own novena etched to skin, inmediatamente.

"One day, mijo, you will have La Madre art like your tío Hector."

No ink, Isaac. Not inmediatamente, not ever.

Hector makes known his protest following Isaac, who is on his way to your lap and clearly confused about the infield fly rule. Out of all the things to happen during the game, you never thought a purposely dropped infield fly, with men on base, would grapple your son's attention. Isaac doesn't think it's fair to be automatically out at any point. He hates the infield fly rule, but you don't press it too much, so as not to distance him from the game. Hector would like to challenge you about his place in Isaac's life, out of pure determination to dominate you in your own home. This interruption is madness! Blessed Mother herself: Mariana dancing for Dodger luck in the kitchen. She has on her favorite game shirt, which has *Dodgers* splashed across the front as if flicked from a paintbrush. It is game-worn and thin enough to make out the dark skin of her sloping breast. Pressing.

The rabbit ears demand your attention and Isaac expresses amusement in the bouncing jaggedness of the reception. Manny Mota and Rick Monday, in left field and center, bent like taffy. You tell him to pay attention to the game, to anticipate the next play.

"Mijo, there are two outs and a man on first and third. If a ground ball is hit to you at third base, where are you going to make the out?"

"I don't like third base," he says.

You explain that third base gets all the action. "It's the hot corner," you say. "The place where the ball dances like fire," you say.

Isaac looks at you with his arms crossed. "I wanna be in the outfield." He sits up from his Indian-style posture and places a finger at the top of the screen on Dusty Baker, who looks clearly bored to tears, filling the void in right field. The outfield—there is so much fat in the outfield.

He tells you this without knowing what it might be like to be Ron Cey, "the Penguin," as he's better known, because of the waddle in his stride, glove as big as an outstretched wing.

"Watch the game," you instruct, knowing it best to leave him alone at times like this.

Steve Garvey has been up to bat three times and has gone 0-for-3. His nickname early in his career was "Mr. Clean." Dodgers skipper Tommy Lasorda was quoted as saying, *If Steve Garvey ever came to date my daughter, I'd lock the door and not let him out.* That was before rumors of illegitimate children with secretaries and marriage statistics to match his at bats in tonight's game. You steer Isaac toward following the rest of the infield position players. It's the bottom of the fourth, and Mariana comes into the TV room with a look you've seen before. "Where the hell have you been? Maybe Garvey would have made this thing a game." In response, your drunken wife of six years attempts to dry hump the television like a wild monkey in front of your nine-year-old boy. There is no argument that Mariana is bang sexy in the glow of the Dodger at bats. She puts one high-heeled shoe on the television and digs the other into shag, thrusting her bare midsection at Steve Garvey's face. You know everyone at Dodger Stadium can see his grin from the upper deck.

"Come to Dreamer," she screws. Dreamer is her nickname from another time and place.

The count is full, 3–2, and she is blocking Garvey's view of the defensive alignment on the first-base line. Houston's Bob Watson is creeping up the line to cut the chances of a grounder to the outfield scoring Davey Lopes from third. Isaac looks at you with contempt of your love for the Dodgers. This is Dodger Blue. And despite all you think, you are Mexican! You can't help but grab the world and Dodger baseball with your whole heart. Hector completely removes his wifebeater, exposing Our Lady of Guadalupe. Her head bows downward in a deep prayer as all her stars fall to the serpent coiled at her feet. Mariana yells out, "C'mon, Garvey, mi amor, get a hit for Dreamer!" She kisses the television screen, leaving a dark red lip print on the screen. The rabbit ears bend closer to her, eventually working their way under the knot tied into her Dodger tee that you bought her before she got pregnant with Isaac.

Lighted by the television from the back-and-forth shots of Dodger players in their mostly white uniforms, Mariana's breast falls from her shirt—a single to right-center for Garvey and the stand-up tying run, Lopes pumping his fists all the way to the dugout, as though he, too, has caught a glimpse. Your son's self-proclaimed uncles wave their arms in the air and holler in Spanish. You have never been happier not to be able to speak the language. You and Isaac are the only two in the room unable to keep up with the high-speed chatter. Mariana clutches her right breast and turns her attention away from number six to Hector. She finishes his Budweiser. She looks into his eyes, applies more Ruby Woo lipstick, and says, "See what I can do? Dreams come true, no?"

Garvey has a two-step lead off first and is thinking steal.

The Houston Astros have managed their way out of the inning, taking the game into the top of the fifth. Still the game is tied. Pitcher Mike Cosgrove is at bat and Hector flips the TV a tattooed middle finger, the *I* from *VIDA* spelled out across four knuckles on his left fist. Mariana finally leaves to the back of the house to get ready for her night out dancing at Peppers.

Isaac lays out the baseball cards you gave him last Spring Classic—he likes the colors of the East Coast teams more than the West Coast teams. You tell him the Dodgers were an East Coast team. From Brooklyn, you say. When he asks why they moved, you crack a joke about Mexicans and Puerto Ricans. You tell him about the white whale of a man named O'Malley and the uprooted people in Chavez Ravine who began everything here. He looks at you, suspicious about it all. His sex-bomb mother in the back room coupled with an on-screen 5—4—3 double play.

Isaac suggests the two of you go outside and throw the ball around. You tell him to wait until the seventh-inning stretch and sit him down on the floor. You stare down to the end of the hall. Hector is nowhere to be found.

He stands up. "Now," he says, with one hand cupped around the back of your neck. "Play ball with me." These words have never been strung together so neat and hard from your son's lips: *play ball.* Catch in the street may be the only thing that separates the last three outs of the sixth inning—a Dodger lead thanks to a Manny Mota sacrifice—and you changing the landscape and rocket trajectory of Isaac's future by doing something universe altering for Hector. Isaac's timing is an effort to keep you from becoming the Mexican man you are so hell bent on him not becoming.

You agree to go outside with Isaac because you think the boy should not hear the comings and goings of his mother's ways. You don't realize that Isaac is used to his mother's sexual magnetism in Pico Rivera. All things come to this house. Sometimes he even hums to the rhythm and press coming from the next room on the nights you watch the game at Peppers. It is the infield fly rule and the lack of a good baseball glove that has Isaac presently upset as he ties his shoes to go outside, upset that the only gloves available are the ones from your high school days. Although well worn, none seem to mold to Isaac's hand in a way that will protect him from the heat you plan on throwing, low and inside. He pulls out a white-creased, heavily oiled Rawlings from the corner of the garage, and seems content with the choice. But just before the two of you get to the screen door, José Cruz, that bastard José Cruz, takes one deep off Sutton to right field, over the head of a glazed-over Dusty Baker, tying the game at two all.

"Damn it, Sutton." All the interest in going outside has vanished while you watch Cruz thump his chest in a macho gallop around the bases.

"Dad?"

"After the game," you tell Isaac.

"But it's almost dark."

You guide Isaac back through the screen to his spot on the floor. "We gots streetlights."

Your cousins and their indecipherable high-speed chitchat pace the living room during commercial breaks. You get up to grab a beer, and Isaac corners you in the kitchen.

"Why don't you know Spanish?"

"I speak a little," you say. "Honestly, mijo, I don't know why."

Isaac has heard the language the last two-thirds of the seventh inning and has picked up on the basics.

"I want to learn Spanish with you. It's not hard."

"So learn it." You shoo Isaac from the kitchen. "Go ask your mother."

Isaac steps back and looks down the hall. "She speaks it already."

Hector pulls on your 1974 Western Division Champs T-shirt from the dirty laundry in the garage, blanketing an oversexed and underpaid Our Lady of Guadalupe. He overhears the end of the conversation and says the only real way to understand a culture is to know the pop in its language. He says this kind of shit to your son until the bottom of the eighth, a few times pointing to you across the room. "You come live with your tío. I'll teach it to you. Your father is too flojo pendejo to teach you."

Hector goes outside and rolls a smoke.

Mariana walks down the hall and into the bathroom. After a few minutes, she comes into the living room and pulls and twists her hair into a tight bun at the crest of her skull. She shakes her head at Isaac when he takes his batting stance in the kitchen. He swings from the wrong side of the plate and tells his mother how much he wishes you spoke Spanish.

"I didn't marry *Chico* here because he's Latino kick-ass. Knew that much," says Mariana. She brushes her hands through Isaac's hair and pulls him into her arms: this is how you love her most. She whispers in your son's ear, "He was supposed to be a big-time player." She says, "Shit, he ain't no number six. Right, mijito?" Then she kisses him with that mouth.

You played varsity baseball at Cantwell with your eyes closed. Played third base like a man on fire, with the hops and glove speed to pluck line drives from thin air. A defensive dynamo down the line, you were. The San Diego Padres scouted you your first year at UCLA on full scholarship—prodigy, they touted. You played in their farm, always keeping one firmly planted foot at the corner of West Hammel Street and Gerhart Avenue. It's where your lucky horseshoe hung. Your first year you had 92 hits in 343 at bats, a slugging percentage of .440. Then one game you swung for the fences with bases loaded in a game that meant nothing and got numbness in your throwing arm that sticks with you today.

Mike Cosgrove strikes out the side and is going for the complete game. The Astros have the top of their lineup due to bat. Mariana struts herself across the living room right under your nose. She says under her breath, as if to seduce you, "I don't know why they aren't winning. I did all the Dreamer I can do." She joins Hector in the backyard as he licks the fine paper edge on her rollie.

The reception on the TV makes the top of the ninth barely watchable. Tommy Lasorda is stretched out like a nineteen-inch pancake as he walks onto the field to relieve Sutton. He is tapping his left arm, calling to the bullpen for the closer. He wants lefty Stan Wall to face Cruz, who is 3-for-4 on the night. Hector has had enough of your TV and suggests a trip to Rafael's for carnitas and beers. Mariana grabs her purse and tells you she is going out with her sisters for the night. She walks out with Hector.

Gets into his ride.

Isaac is asleep and has been since the start of the ninth. Just as well. You sit down to watch the end of the game. Before you can put your legs up, the first splitter out of Stan Wall's hand towers high into the night sky above Dodger Stadium. You imagine the ghosts in Chavez Ravine throwing it back over the fence.

Cruz's second home run of the night is the knife in your belly.

"Ah hell," you say out loud while turning off the TV. You move to the other end of the house so not to wake Isaac, and go to the bedroom to get the radio off the dresser because the reception has now gotten so bad. When you turn it on to see if the batteries work, a buzz swarms through the house. As you walk out of the room, you see the box marked *Dodgers* in black marker sitting in the corner, the box with a picture of Bill Russell on its side. You stack the radio on top and take both to the kitchen.

The AM reception of the radio is worse than the TV. You can barely make out Dodger broadcaster Vin Scully's voice. It cracks every few seconds as he announces: *Farmer John's hot dogs, Dodger Dogs, proud sponsor of Dodger baseball.*

You open the box and step away to look out the front window to where Hector's car was parked. It is important that everyone is gone. Using two hands, you take out the bubble-wrapped items. The arrangement is meticulous. Nothing out of order. There are Station 76 collector pins and lithographs. Championship team photos and ticket stubs dating back to '58, when the Brooklyn Puerto Ricans called it quits. These are the Dodgers of yesterday, your father's and grandfather's. The items here on the table mark an exact time—in some cases, a very specific moment—in Dodger history. If you really think about it, you can say you were Dodger fan before you were Mexican. "This is *my* language," you'd say to Hector, clutching an autographed 1963 championship baseball in your strong hand.

It's the bottom of the ninth with one out, and Vin Scully announces Rick Monday's return to the plate. There is a man on second, but because of the radio's reception, affected by all the pots and pans in the kitchen, it is impossible for you to figure out if it's Cey or Lopes. The Dodgers need a good baserunner with the winning run up to bat. Lopes will make it home on a single to anywhere in the outfield. The Penguin will only make it the ninety feet to third.

You pick up Isaac from the couch, waking him. "Let's go listen to the game outside."

Isaac rubs the squint from his eyes. "It's too cold out there," he tells you. "Watch it on the TV."

"It's busted. C'mon, we'll sit in the car."

You take the items off the kitchen table and pack them back in the box.

"Here, hold this," you order Isaac, so you can grab a couple of jackets. He backs up and shakes his head no. You crack the box open. "Check these out," you tell him. "Go ahead and grab something."

He targets Zimmer and Nen, Koufax and Drysdale.

"These smell old," he says and pulls his head away. "Like dirt."

There is a chill in the air that Pico Rivera has not felt in some time. A thin layer of frost covers the windows of your 1976 Honda Civic. "I'll start her up and get the heater going." You set the box down in the front seat between you and Isaac. He rests his head against the passenger window. He expels bursts of air through thinly pursed lips like the smokestacks downtown.

The car starts and the radio blasts, straightening Isaac upright in his seat. He reaches for the volume and turns it down.

"What station is the game on?" he asks. "Wait," he continues, "I know." And as soon as he tunes in the game, Vin Scully's excitable voice marches out from the dashboard. Rick Monday has put the ball in play, and Astros third baseman Ken Boswell bobbles the grounder before short-hopping the throw to first. Cey *is* the baserunner. He barely makes it to third in a headfirst slide. Vin Scully describes Cey's slide in the broadcast as he calls time out to wipe the dirt from his chest.

"What luck!" you call out, slapping both hands on the dash. "That's okay, we're still in this."

"Who's up to bat now?" Isaac asks. It excites you that Isaac's not being able to see the game has made him interested in its outcome, that somehow his senses have been heightened. "I bet it's Bill Lopes," he says.

"Russell," you correct him, "Bill Russell, Davey Lopes." Isaac looks to the floor of the car after being corrected, losing some of his excitement between the cracks of the seat. You yell out, "C'mon, Bill Lopes," bang the inside roof of the car, and begin poking Isaac's ribs under his jacket. Isaac laughs and reaches into the box. He pulls out a yellowing autographed baseball. "Can I hold this?" You shrug your shoulders and breathe in deeply because you are now *this* close to planting the Dodgers in your son.

Runners are at the corners with one out. Dodger catcher Steve Yeager steps up to the plate. He takes the first pitch and drives it foul into the left-field stands.

As he did with Hector's tattoo of Our Lady of Guadalupe, Isaac now traces the signature on the baseball—*Best, Gil Hodges*—distinguishing ink from lace and leather. He pretends to lick it just to see if you're paying attention, and then tries to replicate the signature on the frosted passenger-side window.

Yeager steps out of the batter's box and is playing mental games with the pitcher. The next pitch is a curve that doesn't break. It sends Yeager to the dirt. Isaac tosses the ball back into the box and sits for a moment, listening to boos coming from Dodger Stadium over the radio. He reaches in and takes the ball out again.

"Catch?"

"Sure," you say. "Let's do it." And Isaac is first out of the car.

"Leave the doors open so we can hear the game."

He walks off the curb into the street and hesitates in the well-lighted neighborhood as the night air smacks his face. He shudders, and you think Isaac might be having second thoughts about playing catch. But he turns to face you and hides his grip on the ball in his oversized winter coat. You expand your chest and shift your weight directly over the balls of your feet, like a catcher hovering over home plate. Pointing your index finger straight down between your legs, you give the sign. Fastball. Isaac waves it off and steps onto a pretend mound. You aren't even sure he can make the long throw from where he's lined up, four car lengths down the street. He leans in from the stretch to start his delivery, and looks to the parked Honda as it leans toward the steal. He throws a perfect slider. It starts out like a high fastball, seams spinning downward, and then bottoms out into the asphalt two feet in front of you.

Isaac signals you to move to the curb. "Car!" he calls out, pointing to the headlights coming your way.

The autograph is scuffed, *Gil Hodges* reduced to a last name. The leather is wet, and twenty years of dust turns to a light viscous mud. You pull at the seams. The casing starts to pull away without too much undoing. You try to wipe the mud from *Hodges*, but the signature smears under the pressure of your thumb. So you pack it like a snowball in an effort to return the throw.

Isaac steps off the curb and waits in the street. He rocks his hips back and forth. Vin Scully is doing postgame interviews from inside the car, and you don't even know the final score. You ask Isaac who won the game. He dances under the lights in the Big Show. "Bill Russell, Davey Lopes, Bill Russell, Davey Lopes." And suddenly you feel the sixty-foot-six-inch distance between the mound and home plate contract in an unrivaled chill.

HOMEGIRL WEDDING

Today is Shy Girl's wedding. It is a March wedding. This means I can show everyone in attendance the bright star Spica in Virgo, or introduce them to the Small Magellanic Cloud that is in the constellation of Tucana. It will take some imagination on their part. I will point out Canopus—the second-brightest star in the night sky. If everything goes to shit at the reception, I will keep the ninth-brightest star, Achernar, tucked away in my back pocket. I track the night sky for a living, all its celestial movements, and write down where they will appear ten, fifty, and one hundred thousand years from now. It's simple math, really, so long as we keep spinning the way we do.

My girl Carmen is the celestial body of all celestial bodies. She uses the word *cholas* to describe Shy Girl's bridesmaids, a roll call of middle-aged women that includes a La Lista, a Thumper, and another named Crazy Silvia. I make a face that suggests to Carmen something foul smelling. She says it makes her sad that I look down on that part of her life. I don't look down on it. I just don't know it, and I forget what it means to grow up in Boyle Heights. I grew up eleven point two miles away in Pasadena. It might as well have been one light year between us. She suggests I get a firm hold on the whole cholas thing, that I should practice in the mirror saying it over and over again until it sounds as normal as *cat*. More importantly, Carmen reminds me that I could get my ass kicked for less at this wedding.

"I used to be one, Chris," she says.

"A bridesmaid?"

"You know I used to be down with my girls."

"Don't say it. Please."

"Cho-la."

"What does that even mean?"

"It means I'm from *somewhere*."

"I see." The wedding is sounding much more complicated than the invitation ever let on. "I've never been in a fight," I say.

Carmen rolls her eyes and feigns a lunge with two clenched fists.

"I don't want to be hit in the face today," I say. "And the older I get, the more difficult it is to think that I could at some point."

Carmen agrees.

"Did you date a lot of guys who got into fights?" I ask.

"All my boys fought," she says.

I wish she had phrased it differently. The way Carmen says *all my boys* makes it sound contractual. That somehow she still has their papers. She has fought and has a scar on her shoulder from a knife fight over a broken compact mirror to prove it. I date a girl who has been in a knife fight, and no matter how many times I say it, it still sounds otherworldly to me.

It's been a while since she has been back to her old neighborhood. And even though she hasn't spoken to most of her girlfriends in some time, Carmen says it'll be like going home. She pulls me in and play-fights. I wrestle her to the ground and pin her. Her arms are spread out wide and I am sitting on her stomach. I can feel her legs kicking behind me and I am surprised at how much strength it takes for me to hold her in place. It is as if she's letting me get the best of her, that if she decided to teach me a lesson, it wouldn't take much undoing.

"Well, you aren't one now, right?"

"Chris, let me up. I have to start getting ready," she says. "And you said you'd clean up the yard."

She pushes me off with ease, as I suspected she could.

"I don't do that anymore."

It is just getting warm enough outside that all the dog shit piles are starting to smell. I promise Carmen I will get it picked up before we leave. I put it off as long as I could and neither one of us can take it much longer. It is getting into everything, the way a sealed loaf of bread takes on the flavor of bananas rotting in a cupboard. But it wasn't until I started seeing the Belt of Orion in the constellation of shit on the back lawn that I surrendered to the task. The dogs are gone. We had adopted them from the pound when we moved in, thinking they would help push us toward the family unit we had been silently suggesting to each other. You know how it goes—making comments about babies in shopping carts, or holding a pair of baby shoes in the palm of your hand and daring your significant other to not say *aww*. Carmen did everything with the dogs by her side. She napped with them at the foot of the bed when I worked. She took them for walks twice a day and fed them nothing but the best—the dog food they keep in the refrigerated section of the grocery store. She bathed them and sang duets with them. And then a month later, when they took off under the hole in the back fence, Carmen acted like they never lived one day with us. As though their leaving was some kind of commentary on what they thought of her as a mother. She never said one word about them after that.

"Are you sure you want me to clean the yard?" I ask. "It's all we have left of the children."

"I'm over kids," she says.

She's lying. The topic doesn't dominate our relationship, but it floats around the room like wispy fingers of smoke when the two of us are trying to think of something to talk about late at night. She comes from a big family, so I understand the calling to fill the house with new bodies. I suspect she is lonely, which is why I don't make a huge deal about going to this wedding today, especially since she needs a refilling of something she's either willingly poured out or spilled all over the place.

The neighbors will complain if I just throw all this crap in the back alley, so I tear apart the garage and find two used garbage bags and the empty flat-screen box I wanted to keep in case we moved. I line the box with both garbage bags and fill them. The box seems sturdy enough, but when I pick it up on each end, it is heavier than I anticipated. I tie the bags off and lean the box on its side to tape the bottom. Here is what looks like a brand-new television. Carmen peeks through the bedroom curtains to see me laughing alone in the backyard at the shit-filled television box. She shakes her head and points to her watch. From here I can see how beautiful she looks. She is framed in the window just off center, like a portrait I might hang right there on the side of the house, if I were a man who'd do such a thing. The lawn, however, has seen better days, now peppered with patches of yellowed dead grass that gives it the polka-dot effect of a hundred rocket launches.

We've never looked this good together at the exact same time. Her dress is bronze and low cut at the top and bottom. I don't mind showing her off, and have even gotten a thrill when she bends over in public and shows her ass, making a businessman choke back his latte, or a teenager witness the blast of his future. I take Carmen's hand and lead her down the stairs to the patio where the television box sits.

"I present you the wedding gift," I say.

"That's our TV," she says.

"Well, sort of our TV. Look." I point out over the lawn. "The yard's clean."

She looks at me and then to the box, then to the yard and then to the box, and back to me. It goes like this for a moment. Box. Yard. Me.

"We aren't gonna take that to——"

"No," I say. "No, I just need your help getting it in the back of the truck. We'll find a Dumpster on the way, and I'll throw it out."

Her look wants to know how I can be so technically educated and circus clown at the same time. There is a scientific explanation for this very phenomenon, but it escapes me.

"Look at me." Carmen holds her hands up, and I take notice of her nails for the first time. They are fake and extend two inches off the tips of her fingers, midnight blue with a rhinestone in each corner. She laughs out her nose. "I can barely open a door."

"Fake nails seem a bit much," I say.

"Not for my homegirl's wedding, they're not."

"You are really getting into this, aren't you?" I realize how unsupportive I sound.

Carmen gets up in my face. She slips one of her talons under my shirt button and pulls me in. I've never been this close to her with my eyes so wide open. Even during sex, when our faces are this close, I always close my eyes to picture her under me. "You make it sound like I'm playing dress up with a bunch of my girlfriends," she says.

"That's not what I meant."

"Doesn't matter what you meant," she says.

"Not what I meant, my darling." I serenade her from the lawn, walking around the box. Shit is heavy. I hunch down and isolate my quads to squat up the box onto the tailgate. It slides easily to the front of the bed. Carmen gets into the truck and puts on her seat belt. Her face fills the side mirror as she looks back at me before applying more makeup. Unfortunately, the straps are behind the seat in the cab. I open the driver-side door and explain to Carmen about the straps and that I really should secure this thing because if it goes, it will be about the worst thing that has ever happened. She leans forward without missing a beat or saying a word. I ratchet it down until the rounded corners bend inward and then call it good. I take a minute at the back bumper to straighten my tie and watch Carmen put the finishing touches of mascara on her right eye. And then Hubble's law splits my head in two. It's the law of physics that states that the farther a galaxy is away from us, the faster that same galaxy is moving away from us.

"That one," says Carmen, pointing to the full Dumpster behind Newberry's. "No one will see you."

I'm worried that I'll drop off this box and someone will get my license plate, find out the box is full of shit, and then I'll get a ticket. The sign on the Dumpster reads, *Private Use Only—Violators Will Be Prosecuted to the Fullest Extent of the Law.* That seems extreme.

"No one gives a shit, Chris."

I don't state the obvious. "Let me drive farther down the alley," I say. And there is nothing but full Dumpster after full Dumpster after full Dumpster. "The Plaza del Mar behind Saint Thomas Aquinas has high walls. We can go there."

"We're going to be late for the reception," she says. "Can we please just go? You can take it tomorrow."

I reach through the cab window and pull at the straps, shake the box a little. I adjust my seat and pat Carmen's leg. She jerks it away but then relaxes into the idea of starting the day over from right now. I turn down the rearview mirror as far as it will go to keep an eye on things in the back of the truck.

"All right then, she's coming with us."

Carmen's parents divorced when she was girl, and that is the reason we are only going to the reception. She doesn't believe in marriage—a dog and pony show she calls it. She even hates television shows that spend too much time on big wedding episodes. "We watch this shit to get away from reality, right?" she had asked me when Ross and Rachel got married on *Friends*. Ross had been married three times on the show, and each time I did my best to defend his position to Carmen. I told her that Ross was a man who boils with love. Truth is I felt some sort of kinship to his enduring, and incredibly pathetic, paleontologist character. Love was to Ross an unearthed fossil that he wanted to display in his heart. I knew how that felt, always arranging the smattering of light from burned-out stars in the part of my brain that held things the longest.

Carmen's father moved to New Mexico to work for his cousin repairing air conditioners. Carmen says his mistress moved there first to be with her own children, and he simply followed. A one-way ticket stamped out of Boyle Heights! Broken air-conditioning units were just a big check mark in the pros column. Carmen moved to Monterey Park to live with her mother, who had moved in with a sister and taken work as a seamstress for a bridal shop. This is where I first met her. She was an undeclared student at East Los Angeles College. A colleague of mine, David Bell, taught astronomy twice a week and told me about this hot Latina in his class who he wished he could get down with but knew that the teacher-student relations code suggested otherwise. "But you. It couldn't stop you," he had told me. The deal was I had to tell him everything. "I want to smell that chola on your fingers when you're done," he had said. It was discomforting to be sure.

Currently, I am the director of the Astronomy and Astrophysics Education Program at Griffith Park Observatory. It is a good title but an inflated one, and one that is asterisked with a comfortable sense of mediocrity. You see, back when I was a graduate student, I harnessed more potential than any of my instructors had seen to date. In the end, I think I left them underwhelmed, doing just enough to get enough. No real big bangs as career trajectories go.

I told David to offer extra credit points to any of his Intro to Astronomy students who came to the observatory to hear me lecture on dark matter and black holes, and more specifically, a hot Latina who may or may not want to catch a bite to eat afterward, late at The Hat. When I told David that all I did was look into her eyes as I explained all the unseen matter in the universe, and how it is only detectable by its gravitational effects on other bodies, that all I did was pause long enough afterward to allow for something uncomfortable to happen to everyone in the room except for the two of us, he slapped himself across the face, wondering why he didn't just do the same.

"You're too close to your work," I had told him while sorting through a stack of graded tests on his desk. "If you want, I can review with you how seldom the planets align." And even though he has detailed every woman he has ever slept with to me, I have never once told him how Carmen's sweet taste sits in my mouth for hours.

We turn onto Evergreen, and there's zero curb space from one end of the recreation center to the other. I find a spot in front of the service entrance at the far end of the block. Shy Girl's mom lives across the street in a turquoise two-story split duplex. At least the bars on the windows are decorative, wrought iron with the family's initial at its center, G for Gutiérrez. As for the rest of the house—it looks well cared for, but the age and no other real desire to make the place look spectacular shows.

The car in the driveway is a 1965 Impala—one of the shining arrows in the Chevrolet quiver. Carmen tells me it is Lonny's car. The groom. I want to ask her if she ever dated him, but I don't want her to break out her file folder of past partners. It is lowered down to the ground and rests on a collection of small rubber pads that the groom must carry everywhere he goes. The paint job is pearlescent white with Emerald City green that trims out the whole car. It's a clean ride, but the practicality of it all escapes me. The upholstery has a fuzziness that reminds me of my favorite childhood chair, a chaise that was always my grizzly in the middle of the living room. Lonny's choice in wheels is exquisite, however. It's as though Midas himself owed Lonny a great favor, and to pay him back, he simply walked around the car and touched each wheel before calling things square.

Two girls squeal at one another and string white paper flowers along the side of Lonny's car. One girl is dark haired with high pigtails and in a satin dress with an oversized bow at the back. The corners of her lips are stained orange and her face is red with the blood that screaming brings. The second girl looks sick. Like it has been her whole past and future. But it doesn't stop her from keeping up. They coil each other with the flowers until they fall onto the grass and get yelled at in Spanish by a large woman sitting on the porch and wearing a wide-brimmed hat that presses against the two wedding guests at her sides. I help each girl up from the lawn and nod to the woman, but she has already looked away. Even the sick-looking girl has the strength to pull away from me. She is wearing tap shoes that cause a terrible scratching sound on the sidewalk gravel. She darts up the sloping lawn toward the house with a flower strand high in the air behind her, pulling a lost kite.

Carmen is paralyzed on the sidewalk. I nudge her forward and her calves stiffen under her dress like rebar. She is an immoveable force right now. The only other time I remember her so unwavering was when I told her that the dogs had left sometime in the night, and that if she wanted to, we could drive around the neighborhood and look for them, that they are probably together digging up trash in an alley, that we'd find them in no time at all. But she insisted that these things *happen*. She tried to blame the universe, but I was having none of that talk.

I estimate the crowd at fifty people, and not one has noticed the girl who has come the long eleven point two miles home. I sing quietly into her right ear. "What's our safe word if things start going bad?" she asks.

"Shouldn't I be asking you that?"

She looks overhead at the electrical wires that stitch both sides of the street together. "Possum," she says.

I look up expecting to see one scurrying. "I don't think I could use it in a sentence without it sounding suspect," I say.

"Something else then. Hurry."

"Mention the aurora borealis, and how we are planning to go to Alaska next year to see it for my work."

It's not the best idea because if anyone asks me about the aurora borealis, I will be obligated to teach how ions dance on magnetic fields. The night sky is fucking crack cocaine to someone like me. She doesn't say no, but before she can say anything, Shy Girl spots us tying the loose ends of social espionage. She is wearing a white, lacy, off-the-shoulder gown that cinches her waist before jutting out cylindrically around her very plump ass. And much like a fat man being called *flaco*, or a hairy man, *pelon*, Shy Girl is the loudest and most domineering personality in Boyle Heights. She screams into the house. The two girls run out and jump off the top step of the porch with a pair of scissors. Everyone is looking now.

Shy Girl's makeup is a palette of questionable decisions. Her eyes are smoky, seem almost branded into her face and crowned with baby blue, permanently affixed like a forgotten neon sign in a bar window. I didn't realize black had so many shades. The rose of her cheekbones is underscored with a fine decorative white line that separates her face into a true north and a deep south. I want to blend it in, or smear it, lick my fingertip and erase it completely from Shy Girl's day. Her beauty is best described as durable. Her lips are a shade of red that NASA had to invent. The poor girl can barely stand in her stiletto wedding heels as she trips forward into my arms, clawing at Carmen for support. The large woman on the porch looks up at me, then away again. Up close, I can see that Shy Girl has no eyebrows except for what is drawn over her eyes.

"I'm Chris," I say. "I'm here with . . ." And for some reason, I cannot recall my girlfriend's name. It is as though I am searching for her chola moniker in my head, that her friends don't know her by Carmen, but maybe by something else, like Diabla or Peanut.

"Letty!" Shy Girl screams, and hugs Carmen. Of course. It's Letty, short for her middle name, Leticia. Shy Girl is quick to dismiss me, and it seems like it might just be the free pass I am looking for, a territorial E ticket of sorts that allows me to eat the food here but keep no permanent place at the table.

Carmen is relieved to be welcomed so warmly. I'd go as far as to say that she is already a quarter full. They go back and forth, calling each other homegirl and commenting on how firm each looks, how Shy Girl couldn't be happier with her tetas in this dress, and how that makeup must have taken the whole afternoon, how her tía does it professionally, for reals. Carmen is showing off her fingertips. She points to my truck and pretends to lift something heavy over her head. That's when Shy Girl starts looking around the yard. She focuses on the heart-shaped piñata being tethered to the low-hanging telephone line by Lonny. He is much older than Shy Girl, in his forties and muscular. But his body moves slowly under its own weight. The sick-looking girl is scouring the yard just beneath the piñata. She picks up different lengths of sticks but decides on none of them. Lonny bends down to her and points to the garage. She licks her palm, smacks the top of his bald head and laughs before running away. Lonny eyeballs the space where she was standing like he is expecting to see traces of her ghost.

"Lonny!" Shy Girl calls out. "Come meet my Letty girl."

Thank God. They didn't date. The introductions go on for a while. Some of Lonny's boys come over to say what's up to the girl they have only heard about. Others grab Carmen from behind and spin her. She kisses a groomsman on the mouth by accident when he turns at the last second to catch her lips. Everyone laughs. Lonny watches me from the hood of his showboat car. Really, what am I going to do about it?

I wonder if Carmen is sad she left here. You hear about all the bad things that happen in neighborhoods like this—and I am sure bad things do—but the layers of protection here are like the age-old rings of a great oak. I know Carmen better than anyone here could possibly ever know her, and I know that she would've been fine.

A rail-thin woman wearing red jeans with a large hairbrush in her back pocket walks up to Carmen and Shy Girl and starts to argue about why this bitch, my Carmen, was invited. Her elbows are bony stingers out the back of her arms. Her chest is flat like a fourteen-year-old boy's. If you lined up ten bitches in a room and told me to pick the one this woman was referring to, I'd never deduce the choices down to my Carmen, but this is the case as Shy Girl does her best to calm the woman. Shy Girl transitions to Spanish in a way that suggests the words she needs have not ever filled the mouth of someone who only speaks English. Carmen speaks some Spanish, and she is listening intently, springing backward at times. I don't speak any Spanish. I suggested to Carmen on her last birthday that we take salsa and Spanish lessons together, that it would be us traveling along at the same speed. We didn't do it.

Lonny is backed away now across the street by the chain link fence that lines the recreation center. His foot is propped up and he is laughing with his groomsmen, letting his new wife handle the situation. A couple of the men whistle and dance. They throw signs with their hands, but I know that none of them are deaf. This goes on for some time until a bridesmaid—I am wondering if it is Crazy Silvia because I so badly want to meet a Crazy Silvia—pulls the rail-thin woman away and pushes her toward the backyard where the reception is starting to gain momentum. There are very old women sitting in lawn chairs in the driveway who don't respond to any of the commotion. The arguing can't be over. I don't think those things ever really go away. Shy Girl stomps around to the back of the house. Carmen combs her fake nails through her hair. I listen for her to tell someone that we are planning on going to

Alaska next year to see the aurora borealis, but she takes her shoes off instead and hands them to me.

"Hey, baby," I say, "isn't there supposed to be dancing?" I step in front of her. "We can leave."

"Did you see all that?" she asks.

"We can leave," I say again.

"Don't worry," she says. "It's long time ago stuff, that's all."

"You still glad we came?" I ask.

Her *yes* is tentative. "Had to see my girl. Let's eat and make the rounds. Then we can go, okay?"

"Whatever you need to do."

Carmen takes her shoes back and holds on to my shoulder as she steps into them. I diffused a bomb, no doubt. The little girls are in the upstairs room above the garage, hanging a bedsheet in the window. "I'll find you out back in just a bit," I say to Carmen. "Just gonna go inside and use the baño." When I ask her whose girls those are, she shrugs her shoulders and steps over a large crack in the driveway on her way to the backyard.

No one who lives here is an astronomer. I know this because I am the only person fighting the urge to constantly look up. I focus better in that direction. Growing up, I had struggled with my father's advice on how to keep my eye on the ball. I was the kid who watched the butterfly in the outfield and who was amazed at the times you could see the moon at high noon. He told me that if I paid close enough attention, I'd be able to see the seams on the ball right out of the pitcher's hand, and how its particular spin would give way as to how the ball would eventually break across the plate. It was the single most undoable thing for me as a young baseball player, to focus while facing an eighty-mile-an-hour heater bearing down on me. If Carmen and I ever have a child, and I for some unknown reason decide to put him through the scourge of Little League, I will explain a successful at bat by taking out baseball's technical impossibilities with the naked eye, and substitute the number-crunching that scientists use to accurately intercept and destroy high-velocity descending asteroids.

If something vanishes into thin air, there is the good chance that all you have to do is look up, and that is precisely how I find the sick half of the two girls—dragging an armful of bedding down the hallway at the top of the stairs. She pushes the door closed in the far bedroom. The frame is water warped, and the door simply creeps back open. The alarm in my head is sounding, a warning as to how this might look to anyone who happens in on me. I can't help myself but to go upstairs. The room is darkened, the setting sun burned out behind flannel sheets tightly pulled over the curtain rod and tucked into the corners of the sill. In the middle of the bedroom hangs a Care Bears bedsheet. It is looped through a wire hanger and attached to the ceiling fan. The print of rainbow and clover-chested cartoon bears is translucent, backlit by the on-again-off-again light from inside. I can see the silhouette of the sick girl under the sheet, holding a large flashlight that in her hands resembles a lighthouse perched on the high cliff of her bloated belly. This is all she does, on-again-off-again, until I step on something that requires very minimal pounds per square inch to crunch under my foot. She turns the light off and gulps her breath back, then bursts out coughing like maybe she swallowed her own spit.

"You okay in there?" I ask.

There's just silence. I step out of the room and look down the hall. No one has changed the music volume. The cadence in the multiple conversations is uninterrupted. I peek back in and the sick girl has pulled the sheet down from the ceiling fan.

"I like your tent," I say. I reattach the hanger. "It is the best tent I've seen in a long time."

"It's not a tent," a small voice from inside says. "It's a fortress."

"Of course it is. I don't know what I was thinking. I see now that this is obviously a fortress. Tents are much smaller." The light turns back on under the Care Bear fortress. "Care Bears fan?"

"I pulled them off my cousin's bed," she says in a way that says I should have known.

"Where's your cousin?"

She shrugs and pushes out her bottom lip.

"You don't live here?" I ask.

"Until my Uncle Lonny's wedding's over."

"Who are your parents?"

"Silvia's my mother," she says. And I am excited to find out if it's Crazy Silvia, but I don't think I should ask. There are things that kids shouldn't know about their parents at a young age.

"They call my mom Crazy Silvia."

And it's amazing how the universe works.

She pokes her head out from under the sheet and turns the flashlight on under her chin, revealing the ghostly figure I imagined Lonny staring at off the side of the porch.

"My name is Marlena."

Marlena dips back into her fortress.

"Chris," I say, and there is no response from inside. The flashlight resumes under the sheet.

"You can come inside, if you want," she says.

"I'm sorry?" I pretend that I didn't hear her because I'm not sure that this is a good idea. The inside of my belly is hot. "Requesting permission to enter," I say.

"You can just climb under," she says.

I pull the sheet in the window aside to check on the wedding down below. The old women are sitting in the same chairs. There are fewer people in the front yard now, which explains the hollers from the back. There is a red plastic cup on the rear passenger-side wheel well of Lonny's car. The owner of the cup is a shirtless, sinewy pup, about sixteen. He is leaning back on the car, perched on his elbows. A young woman is running her finger along his zipper line while he nods to her a *go-ahead*. Her skirt is a tight black sausage casing with suspenders and a short gray jacket. The pup has placed his cup on Lonny's car to claim it as his own under the current promising developments, and I wonder if Carmen was ever that girl, duped into growing up.

"Get in here. I want to show you something."

I crawl under to Marlena shining the flashlight in my eyes.

"C'mon now. What are you doing?" I ask.

"Lay down next to me," she says. She is supine on a pile of crocheted blankets, with her head resting on a *Webster's Dictionary*. She scoots over and pats the space next to her. My eyes adjust back to normal. The skin on Marlena's head is thin like tissue paper or an expensive Christmas ornament you find broken in the bottom of a box, poorly packed the year before. "Look up," she says.

She is waving the flashlight back and forth as fast as she can. She stops and catches her breath. "You know what that is?" she asks. Before I can answer, she whispers *shooting star* into my right ear. I nod and tell her that it looks exactly like all the shooting stars I have seen in my lifetime. She raises her eyebrows and I nod again.

"I want to see one," she says.

"If the city lights weren't so bright, you wouldn't believe what you'd see."

"I love stars," she says. She says she loves stars in such a way that suggests she's given up on a whole laundry list of adventures.

"You are one." Marlena has the same reaction on her face that I had about cholas earlier in the day. I move in closer and hold my hand out for the flashlight. "Finish your soda and give me the cup." She complies with curiosity as I take off my belt. It is going to be hard to explain if anyone walks in, but I do it anyway, and use the pin in the buckle to poke holes into the cup. I exact the placement of the holes the best I can and dry the inside with my shirttail. The head of the flashlight fits the cup with only a slight twist that clicks with a small bend and then back into place. My intent is indecipherable to Marlena, her look suggesting that she has met a lot of liars in her short life. I turn the flashlight upright, presenting her with a homemade planetarium, and all the doubt falls away from her. "We're all made of the stars," I say.

She reaches out for the Big Dipper as I turn the flashlight, making it disappear and reappear again. I make the turn with a delicate lean that sits at twenty-two degrees to mimic this night's sky. I explain that this is close to how the stars will look outside tonight.

"We aren't made of stars," she says.

"I can prove it."

"Prove it!"

She reminds me of what it must be like to have a daughter who wakes you up at three in the morning to ask an impossible question because she just cannot sleep until she has an answer that functions as a lullaby.

"You ready for this?"

"I'm waiting," she says.

"Okay, so there's hydrogen in stars, and it starts clumping together and forming suns," I say.

I take the cup off the flashlight and shine a bright ball on the ceiling of the fortress. She opens the dictionary and turns to *H*. "The sun converts the hydrogen into helium. It does this over and over again until it runs out of hydrogen to fuse. To eat, right? Then it starts in on the helium because all the good stuff to eat is gone." She nods right along with me as though she's familiar with all these consumption models. "It fuses the helium into carbon. You know all living things have carbon. You know that, right? I think most kids do."

Marlena yawns. Her skin is yellow in this battery-fueled light.

"Well, the helium runs out, and it starts in munching on the carbon—*chomp chomp*—assuming the star is big enough." I gesture again to the bright sun on the sheet and suggest that this star is just big enough with an okay sign. "Once the carbon is eaten up, the only thing left is a big ball of iron. And when you reach iron, the star is done for. Eating, or fusing, iron takes more energy than it releases." I grab my gut and explain to her that it's not this way with people. She giggles. "At this point, when the iron is fusing, the star collapses, and the energy rises dramatically, then . . . are you listening?"

She nods.

"Then the star explodes as a supernova, which is the most powerful force in the universe. There's nothing more powerful."

She turns to *S* and scrolls down to *supernova*. She pieces the definition aloud: "A star that sud-den-ly increase-es greatly in bright-ness because of a cat-a-stro-ph-ic explosion that ejects most of its mass."

"Right, that's what I said." I attach the cup on the flashlight and spin it violently. "It spreads all that mass—stardust—everywhere. Then hydrogen, helium, and carbon start to find each other again, and from this, life starts up. You, my dear, were at one time at the very heart of a star. You're stardust."

Marlena takes my hands and slows the light's spin. "My mom told me that we are here because Jesus died on the cross."

In all my years of teaching, I have never had that response at the end of my lectures. And before I can answer her, screams come from downstairs as a herd of wedding guests moves through the house. My belt is off and I am under a sheet in a dying girl's room. What kind of messed-up fuck am I? There is no way I can put together the supernova talk in such a way that will sound believable and simultaneously explain how I can use my belt buckle to create any documented starry night.

Why didn't Carmen just come find me? She'd get all this right away. The yelling is in Spanish and I don't understand, but Marlena doesn't look as startled as she does interested, like the two of us are invisible. She springs up and rubs out the sleep from her lower leg that had been crossed under her. The sheet pulls from the fan and Marlena limps to the window. She tugs away the covering and gasps at the sight down below. The voices are diffuse now, and when I step into the hallway to confront my accusers, there's not a single wedding guest to be found.

Marlena yells down to her mother through a closed window, using her first name. I get back to her side in time to burn the image in my head of Shy Girl in her white wedding dress, her veil streaming up like a mighty fin, kicking the woman in red jeans. The woman appears unconscious as Shy Girl yanks up the lacy trim of her hem around her thighs while dropping her spiked heel into the crook of the woman's neck. Marlena's mother gives a beatdown on the woman's abdomen. That Crazy Silvia. The woman turns onto her side and pulls her arms up to defend herself. Carmen stands aside to it all behind a gathering of wedding guests.

The men laugh behind the chain link fence and cheer Shy Girl on to fuck that puta up. Shy Girl's eye makeup is sweating down her face. The woman in red jeans reaches up and twists Shy Girl's hair back and strikes the side of her face with the hairbrush from her back pocket. It sends Shy Girl tumbling backward. The crowd has created a wall. The old women momentarily look up from their seats to see if the commotion will spill over. Their force field is strong. It is over this man-made wall in Boyle Heights that my Carmen emerges—flies really—over the top of Shy Girl and onto the woman. Carmen straddles her, clamping down with the viselike strength of her legs.

I have no programmed response as I watch my ex-chola girlfriend repeatedly punch and claw the woman as she tries to pull back from under Carmen's legs. I know how useless this can feel. Shy Girl sits at the edge of the front lawn, rubbing out the pain in her face. That white line on her cheek is gone now. Marlena looks up at me to measure how to react, her paper-thin head pulsing. I can only turn and look around the room for my belt. She gives up on me and runs out of the room, calling downstairs for her uncle Lonny.

"Forget Jesus," I say to her as she leaves the room.

By the time I come out of the house, one of Lonny's boys has Carmen pulled away and already sitting inside the passenger side of Lonny's car. The woman in red jeans throws in the towel and stumbles down to the sidewalk to lick her wounds. She turns around and flips a middle finger at Shy Girl, who shines a winning grin back. Carmen has no idea what year it is, and I wonder if I slip my face into her view, will she snap back to now? On the ground are three of her shattered midnight-blue press-on fingernails. I pick them up to give back to her when we wake up tomorrow morning. Lonny helps Shy Girl up from the concrete, and everyone yells like this was part of the closing ceremony. He walks her to the car and Carmen steps out to make room inside. Shy Girl hugs her, and they exchange some aggressive whispering between them.

"Less go for a ride," Lonny says. "I know what will make you both feel better."

He pushes the seat forward for Carmen to get in the backseat. She finally looks around and finds me waving from the other side of the car. She fixes her hair and smiles dimly like she might have broken a promise.

"Can I come?" I ask.

"Of course," she says.

"We can go to Alaska now if you want," I say.

"Just past stuff is all. It's over."

I want to make this easy for her. After watching her lose herself like she did, I feel I have all the power, and the best thing I can do is let it dissipate into something neutral. Lonny looks me over like he's not sure if I can sit in his ride.

"I'm with Letty. Congratulations by the way," I say.

He extends his hand, and I muddle through a bro shake of sorts. "Get in, Chris," he instructs. I look around the yard for Marlena, but she is gone. I look up to the bedroom window, and there is nothing. The sheets are all pulled down. My truck is at the end of the street, and from here I see that someone has stolen the box of dog shit. The straps are cut and draped over the side of the bed. I can only imagine their surprise when they open the box expecting a forty-seven-inch flat screen with HD. This lightens my body.

Carmen leans against me, holding a circular section of white rope. It has knots along its length that remind me of rosary beads. "What is that?" I ask.

Shy Girl turns around from the front seat. "It's our wedding lasso."

Carmen hands it to Shy Girl. "Right, from the ceremony," she adds.

"Yeah," Shy Girl says. "We kneeled at the altar, me and Lonny. Silvia twisted it in the middle like this and put it over us. It's supposed to be like infinity, you know. So that Lonny and me are together forever, you know. That's cool, right?"

"I know infinity well," I say.

"You know infinity times infinity?" Shy Girl counters. "That's what I thought."

Carmen squeezes my leg and tells Shy Girl that it's nice and how she wished she could've been at the ceremony to see it in person, but you know how things are in her head about ceremony. Shy Girl hands me a beer from a half rack hidden under her dress in the front seat.

"Where we going?" I ask Carmen, but Lonny responds instead, reaching into the glove box and pulling out a pocket-sized silver revolver. He hands it to Shy Girl, who then points it at Carmen and me. Carmen laughs. She laughs uncontrollably, snorting into my dress shirt. I am the only person not laughing, mostly because I am the only person in the car trying to figure out if one out of four people get shot at chola weddings.

"We're going to Elysian Park," Carmen says. "We're gonna shoot Lonny's gun."

"I've never shot a gun before," I say, and the laughing stops.

"He told me just this morning that he's never even been punched," Carmen adds.

Lonny adjusts his mirror so that he can look me in the eyes. "We can take care of both those things tonight, holmes."

Everyone is excited by my virginities.

We exit the freeway and head into the park. The road winds up the back side of the Los Angeles police academy. The Dodgers play just on the other side of the hill at Chavez Ravine. There are billboards of Dodger players, old and new. There's Steve Garvey handing a ball to the younger Adrian Gonzalez, and Tommy Lasorda shaking Don Mattingly's hand in the dugout. Lonny turns off his headlights and cruises into heavily forested Elysian Park.

The road ends at the top of the hill in a cul-de-sac lighted by three flickering streetlights. Lonny stops the car and gets out.

"Gimme my gun, Becky."

Shy Girl is Becky. Everyone is showing me something new.

"I'm gonna show you how to shoot a gun, Chris. And if you fuck that up, holmes, I'm gonna punch you in the face." He laughs.

Carmen shakes her head and pets my arm to let me know that he is kidding. For a moment, I wish I were back in Marlena's fortress. "We used to come here back in the day," she says. "We would shoot down at the cars on the freeway to let go after something big happened. You know, to get it out of our system."

"The cars. The cars with people inside," I say.

"You can't hit anything from here, but it feels like you are."

Lonny walks under each streetlight. "This is a Saturday night special. A thirty-eight-caliber revolver you can use close up, you know. But I bet you I can hit that light." He points his gun overhead, squints his eyes, and pulls the trigger. The pop is short and has a concussion that I didn't anticipate. The housing on the light explodes overhead and the sparks spread out just like they do in the movies, hitting the ground and dancing for an almost immeasurable moment, and then they are gone.

"It's your turn, Letty's boy," Lonny says. He tosses me his gun and crawls up onto the hood of his car.

"The streetlight?" I ask.

"The freeway," Lonny says. "We're too far to hit anything. But you can get the feel, you know."

Shy Girl hollers out and stumbles to the dirt. All the beer she has been drinking is settling in on her. She pulls up her dress and climbs onto the hood next to her husband. There has never been a tenderer scene than watching Lonny break the heels off Shy Girl's shoes so she can walk. He kisses away the bruise that has taken over her right cheek. It's hard to even tell the two of them apart now in the darkened street under the shot-out streetlamp.

"Stop worryin', holmes," he tells me, making a gun gesture with his thumb and pointer finger. He throws Shy Girl's heels over an ivy-lined cinder block wall into a nearby drainage ditch. Then he says the most marvelous thing. "Marriage is the strongest bond the galaxy has ever known," he says.

"I'll give you that one, Lonny," I say.

"Go ahead, baby boy," Carmen says. She reaches into the backseat of Lonny's car and comes back out with Shy Girl's lasso.

She steps into the rope ring and pulls it to her waist, twisting it at her hip to form a figure eight. She holds the empty side out to me.

"Get inside," she says. She is closer to me now than ever. This is called a blueshift. It indicates that an object is moving toward the observer, and the larger the blueshift, the faster the object is approaching. I can see us doing this again, coming up here and falling into *our* routine. I imagine getting two new dogs, just bringing them home and pretending they're the ones that left under the fence. Carmen will say *what the fuck are you thinking*, and I'll just keep pitching a squeak toy over and over again until the new mutts drop it at her feet.

"Get in here." Carmen throws the empty loop over my head and accidentally scratches me with her broken fingernails. "Oh babe, I didn't mean to do that," she says.

I rest my head in the cup of my shoulder and take aim. Everything I ever wanted to know about my girl is just off the tip of Lonny's Saturday night special. I shoot down on the Golden State Freeway. It is too dark to see where the bullets are going, but I imagine the miles pushing behind each one to the places we're headed. I fire five times into the passing traffic until the gun clicks empty. No one says a damn thing. There is no swerving in the sea below. Deep down I had hoped for something causal, a rollover or the sound of breaking glass, but everything's moving uninterrupted. All the headlights amass in a comet that skirts the four of us. And if my calculations are correct, this won't happen again for a million years.

HEART ATTACK DRILL

Gramps's slump over the wheel is more convincing this week. The school bus moves about ten miles per hour down Wilcox Avenue, and it is eleven-year-old Denise Espinosa's turn to take the wheel. Marcus's turn at the brake. Denise stands with a leg on either side of Gramps, and bends forward over his back like a gymnast, hands at ten and two.

Nadia Zamora mans the emergency radio. She keeps saying to herself, *Don't laugh.* She holds down the call button, broadcasting her nasal slips and honks down a line of four overhead speakers. She grips the receiver and tangles the coil of the cord around her hand like she is on the phone with Mike Avila, flirting late at night. Under covers. She pretends to turn the radio to the emergency channel, her fingers motioning in circles a centimeter away from the knobs, like she's screwing the lid off a tube of Colgate.

"This is bus number twenty-six. We have an emergency." She hints a giggle. "This is bus twenty-six."

A little drool—play drool, not the foamy kind—comes from the corner of Gramps's mouth. The hump in his back tells everyone he is doing all he can to keep the horn from sounding. We know that if the horn sounds, the drill will either be over or his slump real.

Gramps wants the kids to react to a heart attack without thinking. Like putting on a pair of shoes or eating a bowl of Trix. "Heart attacks happen just like that, kids. You just do. Like fires and flat tires, best to be Johnny-on-the-spot." This is the phrase he will say to everyone just after the drill, when the saliva returns to our gums. Gramps is seventy-six, and he doesn't talk like our grandfathers.

Denise can only turn the wheel to the right because the angle of Gramps's slumped body won't allow her to rotate it left. He monitors her from the pretend dead. She moves over slowly, so as not to ditch the bus, killing first through seventh grade. A tinny voice hopscotches alongs from the backseat—"*Denise . . . is . . . turning . . . too . . . fast*"—and everyone laughs. It is clear Denise wants to go back to her seat, to finish stickering her Trapper Keeper.

Marcus is on all fours with his legs crossed. Ankle over ankle. He is positioned under Gramps's right leg, at the heel of his rust-red boot. His hands are stacked and pressing down on the brake. The other kids shout in an instructional orchestra, *Turn right—brake left, turn right—brake left, turn right—brake left!* Marcus is the best choice for brakeman because his dad drives a rig for Mayflower, though his press on the brake is not steady or even today. Marcus gives lopsided compressions, and everyone's tongue is housed just behind top teeth, aspirating the beginnings of nausea. When he finally closes the gap between the floor and the pedal, the bus comes to a stop at Wilcox and Lincoln. Denise gives the wheel a turn in both directions. She grunts and struggles with the bus's rubber grasp on gravel, then turns the key to quiet the engine. She pushes up off Gramps and lopes back to her seat. Everyone claps. The kids who can whistle, do.

Marcus stands up and brushes off flecks of grease and ferrous dust. He looks through the windshield to assess his work. Gramps mumbles, "You press the wrong pedal and we're *all* goners, son. You remember that." Marcus nods and makes his way down the aisle.

Then the big kids take over.

Ricky S. calls out while struggling with the red handle on the bus's back door, addressing us as *girls*: "All right, girls, leave your books on the seat and line up." He unhinges the lever and the shrill of the door alarm confirms our exit. The look on his face suggests he has just tilted the world on its end. "Girls," he orders. "Smallest in front."

The kid wearing the Green Lantern T-shirt jumps out the back of the bus and turns around to face the open mouth between two released yellow doors. His arms extend out to the first child in line. "Let's move it, you!" he calls out to each of the twenty-three children being spit out the back of the bus. We step off a metal lip and he takes us into his chest. Spins us down to earth. Drill time is the only time the Green Lantern has anything to say.

The sweet smell of rising yeast from Amy's Pastry, half a mile back off West Beverly Boulevard, fills our buzzy heads. And then there is nothing but the tall, sweeping brush of eucalyptus over concrete, separated by a line of city-planted oak that mirrors our single-file stance. Kids are picking the gravel and gum from their treads as we collectively look down the neck of the bus. Gramps's thick still in position over the wheel, his arms extending ever downward. Fingertips, blood-pool swollen.

All of us waiting on the intent of his lean.

THE DEEPEST POOL IN MONTEREY PARK

Tomás suspected Alejandro had been using the key hidden under the fake yucca for over a week now. It was for emergency use only. Tomás had told Alejandro this after the phone call from the airline. The representative had described Valerie's chances of survival as *iffy at best, under the circumstances.* It was odd to Tomás that a trained professional would refer to his wife's disappearance and chanciness at life as one might the possibility of rain on a large, expansive dry plain, or the likelihood of a game-winning walk-off home run in extra innings. The phrase stuck with Tomás for days. It stuck with him up to the moment Valerie's father, Alejandro, walked through the front door, whistling some exhausting tune.

"I can get you your own key if you're staying longer," Tomás said.

"You see this graffiti in the front yard?" Alejandro asked.

Tomás didn't respond.

"They wrote *fuck*, Tomás. On the side of the fire hydrant. *Fuck* in green spray paint. That's not coming off."

"I don't know what to tell you, Alex."

"It's disrespectful."

Alejandro's silver-tipped cowboy boots tapped like ball peen hammers on the walnut floors as he navigated the house. That's the thing with wood floors, Tomás thought, they were an informant of sorts, the way the boards creaked by the stereo and how the tongue and groove snapped in and out by the oversized chaise as built-in snitches.

Tomás had grown tired of the old man. His crevassed dark face shadowed under a derby hat, the same plaid shirt and painter's pants he had worn for seven days. A mule kicked in Tomás's head to get out and explain to Alejandro the depth and width of the oversized hole in his gut, a sadness he could fit both fists inside, and how he just wanted the old man to go on with *his* own life. Even if he was Valerie's father, it was time.

Alejandro walked into the living room, where Tomás had been doing most of his sleeping. He took away several empty glasses from the coffee table. The collection of water rings suggested the dryness of the room and the length of time they had been there.

"I'll take care of these," Alejandro said. "I think today will be a good day. You'll see. It will be a day to start again."

Alejandro nodded until Tomás acknowledged his optimism.

He folded the blankets on the couch and leaned against the large bay window as if he were on display. He felt weak.

"I have a key you can use," Tomás said again as Alejandro left the room.

"I don't need one. The yucca has one, no?"

"I'll just give it to you."

"No es necesario. I'll be leaving soon. It'll be your problem soon enough."

Tomás looked just off the tip of Alejandro's pointing finger, out the front window.

"Did you see that pinche hydrant out front?" Alejandro asked. "It says *fuck* on it like it's the name of the company that made it."

"It's the kids at the bus stop," Tomás said.

"Maybe I will paint it before I leave," Alejandro said.

"I don't think you're allowed to go around painting fire hydrants, Alex."

Alejandro tapped the on the window. "Exact-a-mente."

Tomás felt as though Alejandro was trying to pick a fight. Valerie had done the same thing on occasion, over nothing. Tomás could see her now in her father, in a way he hadn't before. The men hadn't talked about Valerie's accident all week, how her plane had simply been erased away by a barely interrupted ocean on her girls' trip to Los Cabos. It was something.

"One way or another, it is looking brand new before I leave."

Tomás agreed.

"Have you seen my beautiful pool today?" Alejandro asked.

"The pool," said Tomás.

"It is my favorite thing about this house. You know, Valerie learned to swim in this very pool." Alejandro tucked in his shirt then stretched his arms out in a swimming motion, great big telegraphed circles, forward and then in reverse. "The neighborhood would come here to swim. It's the longest and deepest pool in Monterey Park, you know. The guy who built it told me he hasn't seen one longer, or deeper. That was years ago when people were building specialty pools with large plastic rock cliffs. Some people had those swim-up bars and fake lagoons." Alejandro winked at Tomás like they had a secret between them. "I never went to those kind of parties."

Tomás turned and looked out to the pool. It was kidney shaped. He'd seen it hundreds, thousands of times. It ran the length of the yard from the patio just outside the bedroom to the pile of cinder blocks lining the outside garage wall. There was barely enough space between the concrete-lipped edge and the three-foot chain link that fenced in the yard to put a BBQ or a table. It swallowed everything. For the life of him, Tomás couldn't even remember Valerie swimming, or barely putting her toes in. She walked around the pool as if it weren't even there at times, as though she could just walk across it at any given moment. Tomás was the only one who cleaned it. He's the one who had to go to the pool store and buy chlorine, bromine, Ultra Clear algaecide, and pool shock. He'd bought the rafts with drink holders and the best automatic pool cleaner, the Kreepy Krauly Platinum. He had told her that it not only cleaned but also sanitized. He remembered pointing to the place on the box that showed a graph comparing it to other cleaners. She complained it stuck itself in the corners and sucked air like a dying fish. It's not that Valerie didn't swim. She was all-state in high school.

She just didn't ever swim here.

Tomás pressed the bridge of his nose to rub out the beginnings of a headache. He pressed his eyes down hard until the auburn light in the house flashed over.

"We didn't use it much," Tomás said.

"It's so deep you can feel the temperature change at the bottom," said Alejandro. "Tell me, what is the name of that gigante hole in the Pacific Ocean. The deepest hole in the world?"

"The Mariana Trench," Tomás said.

"Yes, that's this pool in Monterey Park. No one has touched the bottom." Alejandro continued down the hall. "You were sleeping, no? I'm sorry if I woke you when I came in. You know, now that I think about it, before all this, it's been since Valerie's mother died that I saw you last. Death has a funny way, no? She always wanted me to fill the pool with dirt, to put in a big lawn," Alejandro said. "Everyone knows that Mexicans and a good lawn don't mix. It's best to have the concrete around, all those cigarette butts."

"Valerie mentioned getting rid of it when we got the house," Tomás said.

"I'm surprised the dump trucks didn't back in here the day I left her mother. But you have the house now, and that is fine, I suppose."

"That's why you're still here, Alex, *your* pool? A fire hydrant?"

"What to do, right? This was my home too—you remember that," Alejandro said.

Tomás surveyed the yard. "Yes, I know, but we also made a home here. We made a good home." He thought briefly to offer the old man a sandwich or turn on the Dodgers game. Instead he watched eleven minutes go by on the microwave digital clock and headed to his room to nap.

Alejandro stepped in front of Tomás and took his arm as he walked from the kitchen. "It needs some work."

⌒

Tomás woke to Alejandro's silhouette just outside his bedroom window, a black figure framed by the brightness of the day. Tomás stared at the popcorn ceiling, the animal shapes that appeared and swirled like clouds in its design. When he blinked, they'd be gone. Alejandro extended his left arm across the pool as though he were Moses, now parting the kidney-shaped Red Sea. He tapped on the bedroom screen. "There's a dog here, no?" With his hands cupped around his mouth, he whistled twice: "Here, girl!"

"We had a dog named Lila," Tomás said.

"I don't know any Lila," Alejandro said. He whistled again.

"*Had* a dog, Alex. She died at our wedding."

Alejandro paused. "Ah, I see. It's strange that I didn't think about it all this week until right now. I knew there was a dog story. I wasn't invited to your wedding, but you know that. So, this Lila took my place? Perhaps it would've been me dead at your wedding, no?" Alejandro laughed something wet out through his nose. "No substitutions."

He knelt down and splashed the surface at the shallow end.

"I'd throw mijita in on this side, and with La Madre as my witness, she would swim the entire length and back in one breath." He held up one finger to Tomás like a promise. "Just one breath. I'd call her Aqua Girl."

"Must've been proud," Tomás said.

"She could've been better, but she never wanted to practice. I put this pool in for her. I remember when the excavator guy came to dig the hole for the pool, I woke up early and came outside with a shovel and dug the hole right next to his front loader, so I could say, *Look, mija, I built this for you.*" Alejandro held his hand just left of his waist. "She was this high, with a swimmer's body. Long like a lizard."

"I had no idea you did all that, Alex," Tomás said.

Alejandro shook his head. "She won some races. I have boxes of trophies in my crawl space if you want them. She found other things to do, you know."

"Still, you must've been proud," Tomás repeated.

Tomás's gift back to the world was redemption, but Alejandro didn't seem to want any of it.

Alejandro coughed. "I said she could've been better, is all." He tightroped the edge of the pool.

"I couldn't swim for shit," Tomás said, leaning the top half of his body toward the bedroom window. "I *was* the anchor in my father's johnboat."

Tomás knew how to keep his head above water. He recalled his father making him tread water the length of the dock at Bombay Beach, where they'd snag tilapia out from the Salton Sea. He'd thrust himself from pylon to pylon, and then back again to prove to his father that he could at least backpedal to the boat if he ever fell overboard. At the end of the day, he would pick away the salted crust from his nipples and from the few hairs he had on his chest.

"No trophies for me, but I could save myself if the situation called for it," Tomás said. He wasn't sure if Alejandro had heard, as the old man stood comatose near the deep end.

"She could make it now, you know," Alejandro said. "If she wanted to, she could make it all the way back to this pool."

"Sorry?" Tomás said, confused.

"Mija. Right to this spot," Alejandro answered. He pointed between his feet. "I'd bet all the marbles in Marble Town that she could find her way back here. I've seen her swim in this pool for an hour straight." Tomás watched as Alejandro kneeled at the pool's edge and pointed into the deep end. "Back and forth. Try it. It looks easy, but shit. I think I told you already that this is the longest and deepest pool in Monterey Park. Not by a little bit, either. The man who built it told me he hasn't seen one longer. That's a working pool man talking, not some wetback."

"You mentioned that already," Tomás said.

"Well, if you think there are bigger pools here, I can assure you of two things in this world. Numero uno, they aren't making any more land in Monterey Park these days. And numero dos, if they aren't making any more land in Monterey Park, then they aren't wasting what they do have building bigger pools here either."

Tomás reached down and pressed on his flanks. He rubbed out a sharp pain that shot like an arrow into where he thought his bladder sat full. He took a thermos from the nightstand and unscrewed the lid. He peed inside the plastic bottle like he thought a trucker might do between two distant stops. He screwed the lid back into place until it made a clicking sound and then set it down on the floor just under the bed.

Alejandro skirted the pool where the space was the most narrow along the fence. A shed sat at the shallow end and had a shape like a Barbie Dream House, with small colonial framed windows on its sides. Its hinges opened the roof at its peak to access all the cleaning supplies. Alejandro reached in and took out three-gallon containers of chemicals and the collapsed telescoping broom for cleaning the deep end of the pool where he said the temperature changed so suddenly. He pulled out a canvas tool bag full of wire brushes used to clean the small concrete pores of the algae that made the pool's edge slippery in early spring.

Alejandro placed the bag by the ladder. He took out several tools and inspected each for wear. Tomás wondered if Alejandro had any idea he was being watched ten feet away. He didn't seem to as he spit on the head of each brush and rubbed the bristles clean with the corner of his plaid shirt. He scrubbed each for a minute or two, inspected each again, and lined them up on the concrete like toy soldiers. He stood and twisted open the broom. With a hard lean on its end, he positioned his hands as though he were preparing to pole-vault himself into the neighbor's yard. Then he coughed violently and Tomás saw the bulging vein that stretched from the bridge of his nose to his scalp. It reminded Tomás of the garden snake he had chopped into bits with the lawn mower the week he and Valerie took over the house. Valerie had yelled something to him across the yard, but it was far too loud for him to hear. The snake had coiled in front of the lawn mower in a standoff, and Tomás simply tilted back the mower and closed down on the snake like a clamshell.

The fully telescoped broom entered the water and cut sharply in a mirage that zigzagged at a forty-five degree angle underneath the surface. For over an hour, Tomás watched his dead wife's father clean the pool, its cement curved edge dipping seamlessly into the water as smooth river stone. This was the cleanest it had been since they moved in. Alejandro used a chamois to clean the tiles of their lime deposits. Tomás thought about how he had never cleaned anything so meticulously in his entire life. *Loving* was the word that came to mind.

The Fourth Street Elementary School bus interrupted Alejandro. Tomás couldn't see the bus from the window, but its screeching brakes were a dead giveaway. Alejandro pulled the broom from the water and stood it on its end against the patio trellis. The noise of children getting off the school bus was a daily occurrence— girls squealed and called each other names, threatened to tell one another's secrets to older boys. A ball bounced with tinny action on the paved walk. Alejandro stalked the backyard, pacing like a hyena just as a plastic soda bottle arched high over his right shoulder and landed in the middle of the pool. It sat upright like every SOS bottle Tomás had ever seen in a movie, ripples and gentle splashes against the tile now lovingly cleaned.

Alejandro walked out of Tomás's view toward the fence line closest to the street, and shouted in Spanish at a group of girls. Tomás did not understand Alejandro, but he felt the concussion of his language twenty feet away in bed. He could hear girls' voices talking back at Alejandro, quick-lipped backchat usually reserved for the older girls. Alejandro walked across the pockmarked concrete back into view and held a nine-year-old girl straight out over the deep end of the pool like chopped bait. Tomás half expected a trained killer whale to rocket from the depths and plant a mammal-fish kiss on her reddening cheek.

"Old man, eh?" Alejandro yelled at the girl. He held her over the water, with his hands slipped under her armpits, in a way that showcased his upper-body strength. "No respect for my property!"

The girl whined.

"Let me explain this to you un tiempo. I'll wait if you need me to." Alejandro's arms did not tremor under the girl's weight at any point. Her body stiffened in a yellow sundress that she pulled down against her thighs, a watercolor print that looked like a field of marigolds, but up close was nothing more than pastel smudges dyed into cheap secondhand fabric.

"You are going to get that basura out of *my* pool, sí?"

The girl squirmed and Alejandro adjusted his grip at her sides. She slowed her fight and nodded.

Alejandro lowered her to the pool's concrete lip. He kicked the canvas tool bag away from him, scattering his brigade of newly cleaned brushes on the narrowest path around the pool, where it settled at the base of the chain link fence. Tomás felt dizzy. His legs were for shit, so he sat at the edge of the bed and watched through the window as though it all were a horror movie. Alejandro bent at the waist, his face an inch from the unnamed girl, commanding her to *get the damn basura out of my pool*. He pointed to the bottle still floating at the pool's center. It looked like a buoy to Tomás, and he thought about Valerie as this girl, swimming out to it and taking the tight line at the turn around and then back again, a task he could imagine Alejandro making her do over and over until her stroke was perfect.

Alejandro took the girl's hand, now holding her with one arm. They spoke too closely for Tomás to make out the exchange of words, and he could only see the girl nodding again, as though there had been a firm plan put into place. The two shook hands in some sort of gentleman's agreement. The girl took off her shoes and stood in her white socks with purple crocheted trim that folded over at her ankles in tight, delicate nautical knots. Alejandro picked up her shoes inside each heel with his thumb and middle finger and moved them out to the front of the ladder.

The girl secured her left foot at the edge of the pool. She looked up at Alejandro, who pursed his lips at her and nudged his chin forward. He controlled her left hand as a rudder, trimming her body out over the expanse of water. And from the side arch of her foot, she stretched out with a gaze that fixed on an imaginary object across the pool, as a ballet dancer might, to control the gyroscopic tendency in her spin, then down toward the bobbing bottle.

"I can reach it," she said.

"This will be the last time you do this, yeah?" Alejandro said. The tiles bordering the pool caught the last of the afternoon light. The open bottles of unmixed chlorine released fumes in the air that burned Tomás's nostrils. Alejandro overextended his reach and struggled with the girl out over the expanse of the blue pool as she balanced off the fulcrum of her arched left foot. "Not in *my* pool," Alejandro said. "This is a good lesson for you."

Twice Alejandro had referred to the pool as his own.

The sound of the girl's face breaking water was an unfamiliar one to Tomás. For two years there had been nothing more than a fine and very quiet surface tension of water that separated what he knew about Valerie and what he knew now about her the moment the young girl's lungs began to fill with water. Alejandro tried catching the girl, but he only bear-hugged the empty space she had occupied just moments before. He stretched his arm down into the pool with a force that only plunged the girl deeper at the very end of his reach. Her yellow sundress floated up and over her head, where it spread out like freshly spilled paint. He swiped at her again. This time he came up with her. The bottle floated to the spill drain on the far side of the pool and twirled on its side with the lapping water tipping it up, then tugging it back again gently. Alejandro set the girl down. They coughed together, and the girl pulled at her dress. Alejandro held her in his arms for at least a minute before letting go. He massaged the vein on his head and reached out to the girl with his left hand, but she had already closed the gate and made her way down Gerhart Avenue in socked feet, down the alley between Newberry's and the row of pagoda-shaped public housing, her shoes left behind and neatly displayed on the concrete as though they were for sale in a store window. Tomás looked to Alejandro for his reaction, but there was none. He just charted the backyard for the bottle, now filled with water and in the catch of the pool's deep current.

Alejandro sopped down onto the lawn chair under the patio just outside the bedroom window. He skipped the chair's aluminum frame along the concrete and crushed a small collection of gravel. Tomás sat up. The screen's one-way tint only allowed for someone inside to see out. Alejandro leaned from the chair and pressed his face into the screen, causing a slight inward bow that stretched the screen from the hardware at its edges. His wet skin puddled against the screen and turned his face black.

"You in there?" Alejandro asked. He blew hard through the screen.

"What the fuck was that, Alex? You could've killed that girl," Tomás said.

Alejandro sat back in the chair—king of the pool, Tomás thought. The old man stretched out and then slid the chair closer to the bedroom window. He wiped his face with his shirt and stared at the pool's edge, now rust colored from the crushed small tool soldiers. "You should watch what you say. I was teaching, and the best way to teach is to show. I'm a good swimmer, you know. Now, if *you* had to save her, well . . . we already talked about that. You mentioned you could save yourself."

"Her father is probably on his way now to beat your ass."

"If he's around, I probably know him. Ten bucks he swam here." Alejandro laughed.

Tomás wondered if Valerie's death still made Alejandro his father-in-law. He wondered how death clipped the lingering branches of a family tree.

"I have done things I'm not proud to say out loud," Alejandro said, trying to see inside. "Tomás, you in there?" Alejandro tapped harder on the window frame.

"You need to leave," Tomás said.

Tomás felt a growing pressure inside his bladder. He reached for the thermos, but it had rolled under the bed.

"I can't see you in there," said Alejandro.

"I said it's time for you to go, Alex."

"I don't know about that. Is something wrong with you in there?"

"I'm fine."

"I think things aren't so fine," Alejandro said. "You should know that I'm not a man of penance."

The daylight fell away from the porch and made it difficult for Tomás to see the shadowy profile of Alejandro disappearing into the landscape of the yard. He rested his arms on the sill and squinted at the dark smattering of changing shapes.

"Maybe I can tell you everything I've ever done wrong," said Alejandro. He pushed away from the screen. "Right now. Right now, we're the two closest people in the world."

Tomás stretched his foot out to reach for the thermos.

"If we can agree to that, maybe I will ask you for forgiveness," Alejandro said.

Tomás leaned back in the bed and pulled the blankets over his body.

—

Lila had eaten a dead jellyfish at the Water's Edge Resort in Santa Barbara the day of the wedding ceremony. She suffered from anaphylactic shock at the hotel bar in Tomás's arms. The bartender had cleared a spot next to the CD jukebox. Tomás told Valerie to enjoy the start of the reception, that he'd be fine, that there was nothing anyone could do about the situation, and that he would find her in time for their first dance. A waitress said she'd get her EpiPen from the break room, but she never returned. Tomás couldn't picture her face when he tried.

"No way, babe," Valerie had told him. "I'm staying with you. This is our first real emergency as a married couple, and there's no way I'm going to leave you. What's happening to her?" Tomás explained anaphylactic shock. Lila's breathing sounded more like she was slurping water from her bowl. He explained how her lungs were filling with fluid as it shifted from all the vessels in her body and into all the free space in her body. He used the word *histamine* several times and explained how they were too late in finding Lila, and that there was nothing anyone could do now.

"Interstitial fluid," Tomás had said to Valerie.

"Interstitial fluid?"

"Lymph. Mostly water. All kinds of fluid besides blood, Val. Cerebral, spinal, but mostly water."

Valerie whispered from behind Tomás like a little girl. "Her face looks like a cartoon. Like it's swallowing itself whole."

He turned his attention away from Lila to Valerie. "It's filling her up like a water balloon. You can say she's drowning from the inside."

The bartender offered to call 911 out of not really knowing what more to do. He mentioned to Tomás that he thought there was a pet emergency veterinarian downtown by the mission but that he couldn't leave the bar to help out. He repeated the location of the veterinarian to Tomás three times, and also how he had to open the place in twenty minutes. Tomás looked at his watch and asked the bartender for some extra towels.

"Why do they say drowning is peaceful?" asked Valerie. "They say it's meditative."

"Meditative? Who says that?" Tomás asked.

"I don't know," she said.

"Really?"

"I don't know."

"People who say that have never drowned." Tomás lifted Lila's bulk onto the bar top. "You ever try to breathe underwater, Val?"

Valerie nodded.

"And you'd still use that word, *peaceful*?"

Valerie shrugged her shoulders and placed her hands around Lila, circumferentially. She held the dog in a measuring capacity to get some sense of what was happening inside her body. "I don't think she's breathing anymore, Tomás. She feels really tight." There had been a slight flex in Valerie's forearm muscles that Tomás burned into his memory. "She's heavier, too."

"The body is a flawed system if you ask me."

"There's got to be something we can do," Valerie said.

Tomás remembered how the bartender had nodded furiously.

Valerie buried her face into the nape of Lila's neck. She smoothed Lila's whiskers back along her snout and released each one slowly to watch it spring back into place. She rolled her into a beach towel that had an oversized cartoon crab holding a child's bucket and shovel. A small collection of sand had gathered under Lila, and Valerie brushed it onto the floor.

"You can go, Lila," she said. Valerie waited for the bartender to walk into the kitchen. He looked at his watch and gave her a sympathetic yet urgent *can we move this along now* look. "Sometimes that's all you can do."

—⟝—

Alejandro walked out from the garage with two cans of spray paint and a roll of masking tape. Tomás watched him cross the yard twice, then back again for two empty moving boxes, and thought that he might be making room for Valerie's car, which was still in airport parking and was going to cost a small fortune. Neither of the two men had thought to pick it up. Tomás noticed the Kreepy Krauly for the first time. It had wedged itself into the farthest corner and made that desperate sucking sound of water mixed with air. He sat up slowly and wrapped the wet sheet over his shoulders. He struggled with the window shade on Valerie's side of the bed and pushed out the screen. The crawl through the window intensified the pain in his flanks as he stepped out naked, his toes webbed out along the porous cement edge.

Tomás dove into the deep end, the side he had watched Alejandro clean for over an hour. He looked up through the water's distortion at the old man, who appeared as an angular, wobbly mass. His lungs burned, and he couldn't stay under too long without feeling the pull to the surface. He came up widemouthed for air, swallowing and swallowing. Alejandro walked around the pool to the faded side of the diving board, nearest the patio. He shook the rattle can of paint and yelled into the water, "You won't find deeper!"

Tomás waded at first to measure his body's response to exercise. The blackness at the sides of his vision slowly expanded to view the pool's bottom sloping grade, and the plastic bottle, far beyond his reach, tipped up and balanced on its neck in a pirouette. His thrust sent him into the shallows, fluid and wholly outstretched. Alejandro smacked the shell of the water with an open palm. Tomás heard this and the metal ball bearing inside the rattle can as Alejandro continued to mix the paint. It was this dullish, flat metallic sound cutting through the viscous fire-engine red that acted as the metronome to his quickened pace through the *ping-ping-ping* of open water.

MINEFIELD

The Saint Jude statue sits in the middle of the breakfast table with his head slightly cocked to the right, looking down on the calendar section of the *Los Angeles Times* like he is doing the crossword. His nose is split in two and his long robe is chipped away behind his left knee like he got hit from behind with a Louisville Slugger. He resembles my uncle the day he came back from Vietnam—one leg missing. Nana counts the cracks on Saint Jude and sighs. There is a flash of joy in her old face at the flame above his head, still-flickering paint-flecked mortar. But the way Nana spits on her thumb and rubs the empty space between his eyes tells me that Saint Jude is about to take a dirt nap.

Ricky walks into the kitchen. He is half asleep and watches me stuff a tortilla with potatoes and chorizo and then sits down. Saint Jude is taking in some *Beetle Bailey*. I hand Ricky a tortilla, but he reaches for the one I just stuffed. "Hell no," I mumble, so Nana doesn't hear me mentioning *that* place. "Get your own," I say. I know I won't get another chance to eat until late in the afternoon when the digging is finished.

I have to chew my food slowly because if I get to the digging too soon in this heat, the grease in my stomach will spill up and burn the back of my throat like acid. Ricky eats faster than he should, but then how would he know not to? He's only dug two holes, and both of those were during the winter months. Nana can eat as fast or slowly as she wants. I have never seen her bury a saint, although I know there are Saint Jude statues under the backyard that are older than me and Ricky put together. This will be my fifth time digging a hole for Saint Jude, all of them in July, within two weeks of my birthday. It's like he plans this as some sort of present for turning fourteen.

"Did you say good morning to your uncle?" Nana asks, stirring eggs around in a smoking skillet.

We answer, "*YES!*" at the same time.

"Don't be little jokers. Put down your breakfast and get into that living room right now before I whack you. You know what to do."

Nana pours milk into our Fantastic Four tumbler. Ricky carousels the cup in the palm of his hand to get a good look at its superhero lineup. He points out the Thing to me, then drinks more than half his share. And with his arms extended, his knees bent in a deep flex, he roars.

"You better get moving," she says.

I give Ricky the *let's hurry up and do this* face. We leave the kitchen, and Nana's left eye follows us down the hallway, the right one still on the cooking.

The living room walls are full of pictures—our mother in the backyard, dancing in a black-and-white photo when she was our age, her skirt twirling, frozen in the air, with Tata holding her above his head, squinting his eyes, and turning his face away to the left, in fear of her propellering skirt. There are Disneyland trips, that fat fish Shamu, and all the birthdays lined up and labeled by year and kid. Here is my baptism. There are pictures of women called Carmelites.

Uncle Joe's picture is in a twig frame and sits on the television next to a box that holds all his war medals. Ricky and I can't watch a minute of *Get Smart* without looking up at him during the opening. He watches over us through the dancing flame of the lit candle that Nana keeps between his picture and the Sacred Heart statue. Ricky calls the Sacred Heart the inside-out Jesus, since the statue is holding a heart outside his body. And much like the top of Saint Jude's head, it is on fire. Piercing through the heart is a small metal sword that slides in and out, and fits perfectly into the hand of the Bionic Man, or snug in the belt loop of his red one-piece jumpsuit when he needs to lift his half-ton engine block. The sword never leaves the living room. That's the rule.

There is more than one picture of Uncle Joe, but this is the best one, him in his army greens. Look here. He is on crutches with a small American flag stuck into his armpit so he can hold up the plate of cookies our mother is shoving into his chest. He had just come home, back from killing. Nana is in the picture with her arms around him, keeping him balanced on his crutches. His right pants leg is rolled up and stapled at the knee. Our mother has snot running down her face, crying and crying. I think Uncle Joe should look happier to be home.

"You say it first," Ricky says, bouncing on his left foot.

"Good morning, Uncle Joe."

"Why do we have to do this?" Ricky asks.

"I think 'cause he got his leg blown off."

"Think he'll ever come back?" Ricky asks.

"Why do you ask that every time? I don't know."

Uncle Joe left everything behind. Nana says he just got up from the dinner table, not even asking to be excused, and hopped on one foot out the back door. He even left his crutch. It's right here where it's always been, next to Tata's old Stratocaster. Mom thought he might have been checking on some of his buddies driving up to the house, but that wasn't the case. He hopscotched outside and got into a Datsun 210 that neither Mom nor Nana knew from the neighborhood, and has been gone ever since. They didn't say Datsun 210, but it's my favorite car, so that's how I tell the story. Mom told us that he didn't even look her in the eye when he left. She said it was exactly what our dad eventually did to her, and that if we ever do that to a woman, there will be hell to pay. Nana says that even though we have never really met our uncle Joe, he's more of a father to us than our own.

Uncle Joe had just whispered something to Nana that night, but no one can tell you for sure what he said because Nana keeps her secrets locked inside her heart. Ricky and I have been living with his ghost ever since. With the one leg gone, I am pretty sure he'd be easy to spot. So when I take the garbage out to the back alley, or run through the aisles in Newberry's, I always keep my head on a swivel for a one-legged man looking for a place to sit down.

Nana is stuffing all the breakfast remains into one tortilla. She rolls it into a paper towel, cuts it in two halves, and holds them out straight-armed for us to choose. Ricky comes in right behind me and inspects the two halves. Nana knows better than to help start a fight. She matches the top of each half and holds the bottoms in a closed fist, choking out chorizo and cheese like breakfast lava. It is difficult to tell which is the larger of the two cuts. Then she says something in Spanish that commands us to make a decision. I am shorted.

"Ricardo," she says, "help your nana. Get the shovels."

"Yes, ma'am."

Ricky waits for the screen door to close, then turns around for me to get the full shot of him taking a bite out of each burrito. He does a victory dance that I have seen before. Nana directs me to wash Saint Jude. I reach under the sink and grab a new sponge from the box marked *Super Kleen*. The water from the faucet will take about five minutes before it is hot enough to use on a saint. I know this.

I put the sponge under the scalding water, holding the smallest corner edge with my pinched thumb and pointer finger so as not to get burned, and walk to the breakfast table, leaving a path of small, steaming droplets behind me. The Human Torch looks right at home now, the steam swirling around his fiery, torching fists.

Nana is counting the cracks that look like hair along Saint Jude's faded robe.

"There's more cracks this year, mijito." I push down on the sponge, and it begins to hiss.

Scrubbing this Saint Jude is similar to how Nana describes her scrubbing Uncle Joe in the middle of the night, back when he woke up cursing those *goddamn leg-taking gooks*. Nana doesn't say *goddamn* or *gooks*. She says *the Lord's will*. Our mom says *gooks* every chance she gets, and I have come to believe that *gooks* means more than one thing or another to her. The scratchy side of the sponge has cooled some, but it is still warm enough to take off the bird crap and sap from Saint Jude's shoulder blades, where everything hits him square. I stop when the last of the paint around his armpits begins to fade away.

"Take the corners of the newspaper, mijo." Nana instructs me on how to best wrap this Saint Jude. His size is never the same from year to year. "No, like this, mijo." She pulls the paper, twisting it above his head like a flower that hasn't yet bloomed. Saint Jude is packaged much like the gold Christmas ornaments our mom gets in the mail every month. There is a stack of the velvet ornament boxes in the back bedroom underneath Uncle Joe's rucksack. They smell musty like the porn magazines Uncle Joe keeps inside. I look at the magazines every chance I get. Lacie is on page sixteen inside *Cherries*. She has a red ponytail and a necklace of white pearls that extends the length of her body. Her skin is freckled and the color of buttermilk. She is outside on a windy day and never looks directly at the camera as she plays and tugs the pearls down between her legs. The caption under her photo asks if I want to be inside her. I guess. I look at her so much that if you dropped the magazine on the floor, it would open to that spot every time. As much as she wants to, Nana won't throw them away. She says that Uncle Joe has to come back for something, and that our Lord and Savior works in mysterious ways.

I know it won't go anywhere, but I can't resist bringing up Uncle Joe. "Nana, do think he will come home someday?"

"What would you say to him if he did?" she asks.

"I don't know what I'd say," I say. It is a question I have never really been able to answer, and it gets harder the older I get. I'd probably ask him what it was like to lose a leg. One minute you got two legs, and the next minute all you can do is think about the things you've never done when you had both. Except hopscotch, of course.

"You were too young to remember him," she says. "And that's why I want you and your brother to talk to him every morning. When he does come home, I don't want you to be afraid."

"I am not afraid of a one-legged man," I say.

She tells me to count my lucky stars, mister.

Ricky is doing his best to juggle the remainder of my breakfast and two shovels in the breezeway. From the kitchen, I can hear when a shovel gets loose, scraping its metal head across the red-painted concrete, leaving a chalky white line that I will have to scrub off when we are done. Nana tells me to stop paying Ricky any attention, just to *something something in Spanish*, and focus on the task at hand. She says she thinks I have perhaps forgotten the importance of burying a saint.

"Saint Jude, mijo," she tells me, "is the saint who comes to those who are in desperate need." I think to myself that this particular Saint Jude is in desperate need of another Saint Jude to come and rescue him. The little fake flame is working its way out the top of the newspaper, ready to ignite the whole damn place.

"Why is Saint Jude's head on fire?" She has told me before, but I get it confused with Jesus's inside-out heart and Saint Teresa's crying roses out her eyes. I read that it wasn't roses she was crying, but the blood she was spurting up from lung disease. I never mention the things I read because I don't want to have to apologize to the Saint

Teresa statue on Nana's side of the bed. This is the first year that I am taller than it.

"Your arms, mijo. Put them out," she orders. Nana pushes Saint Jude into my chest. "I'll get the map."

I rock Saint Jude back and forth like he might start to cry at the noise Ricky is making in the backyard. The force of my grip turns my fingernail beds white, and the blood in my body feels as though it is circulating the wrong direction. My thumb punctures through the newspaper, straight through Magic Johnson's toothy game-winning grin and up Saint Jude's butt. I start to laugh, and I have to take a long, deep breath before I tell myself to stop. I put him on the kitchen counter in a better position to get a look inside where guts should be. My goodness, what a great hole! Had I known he was hollow inside, I would have packed him full of army men a long time ago, extra troops to pull out when Ricky thinks he has me surrounded, would've stored the soldiers Nana took away from me, the ones with all the legs cut off at the knee. Why Nana was so upset is beyond me, asking me why would I do such a thing as to snip off the legs of every soldier with her good Gingher scissors.

"Such a thing to do," she had said.

"Uncle Joe is the only soldier I know, a one-legged radio private." I had him machine-gunning with one leg, throwing a hand grenade with one leg, squatting down and one-legging it under barbwire, past the gooks and the Lord's will. "He's my supersoldier, Nana." For six months, Nana kept my army of Uncle Joes in a bag high up in the garage. The plan was to wait until she forgot all about them and then, under the cover of night, sneak across enemy lines for the covert rescue attempt, a mission thoroughly planned out while watching an episode of *The Rat Patrol*. On an in-service Friday, I came home from school to find my army of Joes melted into a green plastic glob holding open the door to my room. Nana's kiln in the garage is as hot as hot gets, and apparently it takes eight hundred and twenty-five degrees to melt my Uncle Joes into green army juice. Nana believes that we should never forget how we got to our current place in life. That is the exact message she had carved into my waxy new doorstop.

Nana unfolds the map as she walks past me and out the back door. I think about desperate needs, about how Uncle Joe hasn't been home since two months after I was born. Nana says he is alive, but I am not sure what that means. I believe a lot of things.

She says Saint Jude is alive in her heart.

I will never leave here. I am just not interested in growing up and losing a leg. I think desperate needs, and go into the living room to the box that holds Uncle Joe's medals. I open it and finger around inside. The only medal not inside the box is the purple one, which has its own case and hangs on the wall. It is a heart, but not inside out of anything. It is by itself, resting on black felt, on the wall underneath *The Last Supper*. He got it for blowing off his leg. I stare for a while, and it just comes out: "Go and blow your leg off," I say in my deep army general voice. "Clean off, Private."

I slice the newspaper around where I think Saint Jude's face should be and pull back the paper flap. The space where his nose is missing is now clean and white and bird crap–free from its honeycombed cement pores. "Take a look, Saint Jude," I say, pointing at the picture of Uncle Joe on crutches, pants stapled at the knee. "It's way too late to do anything about the leg, but I'll take bets you can bring him home." I finger a little more through the medals before finally deciding on a small bar of silver stars and a circle with two attached miniature rifles that cross one another. "Got this for being a spot-on shot." That's not good enough soldier, I think. "You got it for snapper killin'." I move the remaining medals around in the box to take up the empty space and go into the back bedroom to tear Lacie out of Uncle Joe's magazine. I wrap the medals inside her and push both deep into Saint Jude's hollow guts as far as they will go.

"She'll take good care of you," I tell him.

Nana looks up from her map at me as I walk out the back door. She has a look like she knows—but doesn't know—but knows that I have been messin' around inside.

"Judgment Day. That's all I'm gonna say, mister." She places her rocking chair cushion on the red concrete and kneels down, balancing with the unfolded map. Ricky looks at it with her, pointing out the Saint Judes he has buried—*that one, and that one*. The map is on nine pieces of grid paper taped together. Nana uses our Magic Markers to draw the entire backyard. There is a small orange yucca, purple birds-of-paradise, black rosebushes, and two brown lemon trees drawn on the map like you are staring down on the backyard from the belly of a huey.

Between the lemon trees is a pedestal my grandfather made for Saint Jude back when my mother was a little girl. It is where Saint Jude lives throughout the year, a mostly shady spot that smells of citrus from freshly stepped-on lemon leaves and granite dust. It is the place where the birds bomb-crap most. I ask Nana if that is why we change Saint Jude out so often, but she is too busy working the top back on the green Magic Marker to answer me.

Ricky and I stand at attention on the concrete side of the trim, ready to dig. Once we cross over to dirt, it is Nana's show. She has the thin blue marker out and is checking off the already underground Saint Judes. I count off with her check marks because I badly want to know how many: *twenty-two, twenty-three, twenty-four.*

"How many, you think?" Ricky pulls at my pants pocket to point out the small patch of marked dirt we will shortly start turning up.

Nana is in my periphery, still flicking blue on the map with the slight lift of her wrist.

"At least twenty-four." I tell him some had to be buried under the lawn before there was lawn.

Ricky nods.

"Right here, mijitos," Nana says, her finger pressed against the map. "Start from the first lemon tree and walk three steps to your right."

"Clicks, Nana, they are called clicks. Three clicks." I press my back against the lemon tree after teaching Nana a thing or two about army talk and match my feet toe to heel three times before stopping. Nana is hunched over; her arched spine stretches out above her ruffled shoulders. It is a good dress she has picked out for this occasion, flowing green with bright red hibiscus flowers that look like midair explosions. She blends in with the yard as she hovers over the map to identify the marks in the creases of the lined paper.

"Now take one step back and to the left. Stop two feet from the wall."

"Two clicks?"

"This much clicks," she says with her hands spread out shoulder width.

I move, leaving minimal footprints. "That is perfect, mijo. Now start digging." She pats Ricky on his back, startling him some. He breathes heavily as she instructs him to walk the same path to meet me. "Get in there and show your brother how it's done." His face lights up as though he really thinks he knows what he's doing. I tell him to stay down in a low crawl and watch the horizon for the movement.

"What am I looking for?" Ricky asks.

"Silhouettes."

"What is that?"

"You'll know. But by the time you see it, though, it'll probably be too late."

Saint Jude is resting on the lawn's edge next to Nana. If she picks him up, she might very well hear the medals moving inside his stomach. But instead she just colors like a little girl, a big-fisted grip on the markers as she shades in all the new plants that have grown in around the backyard during the last year. It is important to keep the map up-to-date.

Digging is all about your angle. I know how to properly plant my foot on a shovelhead to run it deep into dirt. Not like Ricky, who stabs straight into the ground, using nothing but his neck and shoulders. I mention this to him, but he tells me to leave him alone, that this is not his first time either.

"Hey, Ricky," I say. "How many land mines you think Uncle Joe walked over before he reached the one that got him?"

"Ten thousand," Ricky says. "I bet those gooks planted a million."

Nana looks up from her map. Ricky might be right, but I bet it was more like four or five on the road he was patrolling, until the pressure of his boot stamped out his leg's future on number six. Nana told us that even in Vietnam, Uncle Joe was probably just being Uncle Joe, doing Uncle Joe stuff, and walking to the beat of his own drum out there in the jungle. I bet he was quiet on that dirt road. I bet he was thinking about Nana's chile verde and the girls in his magazines when he should have been worrying about bouncing betties and the possibility of wearing one-legged Tough Skins from Sears for the rest of his life.

I am halfway into my hole. "Nana," I mumble, "Uncle Joe ever bury a Saint Jude out here?" She stares out over the lawn for what seems like forever and turns back, giving me a look that says she might start to fire up that kiln of hers. It doesn't take too long before the hole is wide enough and deep enough for a saint. Nana sets down the map and reaches for Saint Jude.

"I got him," I say, dropping my shovel and stepping directly on the last twenty-four-plus years of saints.

"Ay, Dios mio!" There's just so much Spanish from Nana at this point to know what to do exactly, so I just do my best to lighten the weight of my footsteps and leap out over the brick trim onto the concrete.

"BOOM!" Ricky yells, and starts laughing, but it doesn't take long before Nana is staring him back down into the hole. He gets low and covers his head to protect himself from all the shrapnel.

She scolds me. "You know better than to do that."

I apologize and check the bottom of my shoes like it might help explain damage assessment.

"Nana," I say, scooping up the statue.

"You know what I'm thinking," she says.

"Yes, ma'am," I say.

"You need me to read the map to you again?" she asks.

"No, I remember."

Ricky steps out from the hole and wipes away the clay and crust from his knees. There always seems to be less dirt to put back into a hole than originally dug out. It's as if someone stole two big handfuls when I wasn't looking. I line Saint Jude's hole with pea gravel so he has good drainage January through March. As I lean down to place him inside, he clanks—enough of a clank to get Ricky's attention. He has no idea that I have stuffed Saint Jude with desperate needs, and that maybe Saint Jude is resisting a bit at the idea of going under. Ricky steps back, a little fearful that Saint Jude might blow up the perimeter. I don't blame him. It took me a few years before I was comfortable putting Saint Jude in his hole. Nana pulls a water-filled mason jar right out of thin air. She instructs me with her twirling finger to pour it over the dirt, which I do, onto a small mound of dark clods that quickly turn into mud.

"It packs well around the gravel, Nana."

"It's holy water from Saint Thomas Aquinas."

"Did you steal that from the jug at church?" Ricky asks.

We never used holy water in the past.

"It's not a jug. It is called the font," Nana says. "Say it, Ricardo."

"Font."

"The font," says Nana.

"The font," says Ricky.

"Father Lynch gave it to us. We don't steal, mister."

Nana prays as we start to throw the clodded soil and a half-opened bag of Miracle-Gro over Saint Jude. I want to tell her that I got things covered. That Uncle Joe will be coming through that gate at any moment. Though it might upset her that I put the medals inside. And honestly, I don't want to spend the rest of my summer digging up the backyard to prove to Nana that it was the first time I ever buried something in a saint.

She holds the map out in front of her and peeks around its corners to exact her drawing. Then she folds it up and tells us to put the shovels away and clean the white streaks off the concrete or else.

"Go inside and wash up. Take off those pants," says Nana.

She hands me the map and doesn't say a word.

I know where it goes.

Before even thinking about lunch, we have to drive over the hill into Montebello and buy a new Saint Jude at Christ's Basement on San Gabriel Boulevard. They have statues there just lined up and down the aisle, ready to take his place. Nana says the next one will be the biggest Saint Jude yet. *One that will rise to the heavens*, she says. And I wonder how big she is thinking, and when the time comes next year, two weeks before my birthday, if there will even be enough space to dig as deep as we'll need in the backyard, where the lemon tree roots are starting to split the red concrete in two.

100% CHEROKEE

Ray warned Felix daily that if he did not get in touch with his Cherokee roots, dang it, all of this would end badly. He warned him of the coyotes, and how they'd been spotted running in packs, and not the pairs Felix recently read about in the paper. Ray quoted their escalating numbers in the Sierra Madre foothills, that it didn't make no darned difference if it were three in the morning or noon, they were hunting—not scared and not resigned to staying in the thick brush of the wash. These coyotes were seasoned. They got the taste of seven-year-old Marisol in their mouths, the deaf girl who lived in the largest house on the corner lot. They got her jumping rope in the driveway one street over, just south of where Felix's family lived on Mira Monte Avenue. They bit at her cheeks. The coyotes took the palms of her hands as she defended herself.

The city of Sierra Madre issued new trash cans after the attack. They were large industrial plastic containers with self-closing lids. Residents had to use them or be fined for breaking a wildlife ordinance that said you couldn't invite coyotes over for dinner. Felix pressed down on the lid to lock it in place, but it would just pop up and bend slightly onto itself, warped from the direct sun that hit the side of the house like a solar flare. Nothing survived on that side of the house. This was the first summer that Ray did not change the direction he parked his '67 Mustang, so that the fading of the yellow and black racing lines would even out. According to Ray, buying the Mustang brand new was his last greatest memory. Felix had eyed the car since coming home early from school. He offered to park it in a storage unit for Ray, or maybe put up a tarp during the summer heat to stop the beating. Ray wouldn't have it.

"Can't go hiding it away." Ray pressed his cane into the long shag strands of the living room carpeting. He looked out the window down on the Mustang. "She's not the worst thing I've ever seen. I've seen more beautiful age worse in my days."

Ray was Felix's grandfather *and* job until he found a real one. There were some weekends that Felix did janitorial work with his cousin Simon's company. This was the only way Felix's mother would allow him to live at home. He cooked Ray's meals and made sure Ray didn't wander off into the foothills when the dementia sent him chasing ghosts. There was clearheaded Ray, and then there was the child inside his head that took over and caused havoc in the house. This was called heading up la resistance. Felix had to hide Ray's dementia medication in his breakfast. Citalopram went in his chorizo and egg burritos. Fluvoxamine fit nicely with the backdrop of hominy and tripe flesh in his menudo. And after breakfast was over, Felix would find it half-chewed and wadded up in a napkin, or simply lined up on the table in defiance, Ray's medications like tiny monuments of victory.

Felix set down a bowl of oatmeal. Ray took out his bottom teeth and placed them on the lace runner that webbed out from the middle of the table.

"No tricks, mijo? I'm an old man." Ray settled into his wide-armed chair with gates that closed on each side like a high chair. Felix had left a gate open the first week he moved back into the house. Ray had missiled into the cherry hardwood floor like he was breaking a land speed record and had to be taken to the emergency room for yet another CT scan.

"No tricks this morning, Ray." Felix cleaned the corner of Ray's mouth after the first bite.

"You can call me Abuelo if it makes you feel better. I know a boy your age needs that. It means *grandfather*."

"I know what it means."

"Then what's with the *Ray* nonsense?"

"So *you* don't forget *your* name."

"Don't even speak Spanish, do you? Try it. *Abuelo.*"

"I'm good, Ray."

Felix wanted to answer his grandfather with some smartass Spanish, but he couldn't string anything together as quickly as he wanted.

"How come you won't do nothing with it?" Ray asked.

This is how the *Cherokee talk* always started, always in the morning when Ray's body snuck out of bed, leaving a note for his mind to sleep in. Managing Ray every day was repetitive, like shooting a hundred free throws at the end of basketball practice. It is the only practical way to getting better.

Felix obliged. "Nothing with what?"

"You're damned Cherokee blood. One hundred percent black crow–haired Cherokee. Look at you."

"Nope. I'm a Mexican, Ray."

"You ain't no kinda Mexican. Trust me, I've known a few."

"Ray, you were born in Santa Rosalía, Mexico. Your father was a federal from Monterrey. Not only that, but you told me that he was a federal who shot a round that ripped through Gustavo Madero's sleeve. I'd say that makes me Mexican."

The words were wasted. "Shit, Sequoyah. How much do you weigh?"

Sequoyah was the inventor of the Cherokee alphabet, Ray's favorite Indian. To Ray, the only Indian. Sequoyah created the syllabic construction of Cherokee language so that the Cherokee could pass on speeches, write books, and read the morning paper before starting their Cherokee day. The giant sequoia trees and Sequoia National Park in Northern California were named after him. The Cherokee seed was likely planted years before Felix was even born, when Ray would take his Mustang through Texas and Mexico, camping along the Rio Grande. But it was just after the coyotes made the local paper that the seed germinated. It was one of the many unpredictable switches in Ray's head that ignited in him a consuming interest in the Cherokee.

Felix sucked in his gut, flipped back his waistband, and lifted it above his navel. "One hundred and ninety-five pounds, Ray."

Ray tapped the spoon on top of his oatmeal like a skin drum. "Not gonna lie, that's a good weight for a Cherokee. Real impressive amount of pounds." Ray admired Felix's bulk from the breakfast table. "Now you just have to learn how to throw it around. This wild dog problem ain't gonna fix itself. Coyotes can't be feeding on little girls."

"Ray, it's not our problem."

"You are right as the desert rain, Sequoyah. Not *our* problem. It's *your* problem, so you better figure out who you are."

Ray pressed his weight onto his rhinestone-encrusted walking cane and took a long rest halfway into his stance. He had the replica cane custom made after witnessing Evel Knievel's famous rocket flight over the Snake River Canyon in '74. When people asked Felix about what kind of man his grandfather was, he responded, *The kind of man who will travel to see Evel Knieval in flight.* He felt it summed up the man well. According to Ray, Evel's cane was filled with Wild Turkey and had a one-karat diamond for every bone the daredevil had broken. There were more diamonds than the number of bones in the body.

Ray took off his black cowboy hat and tapped Felix's straining belly with its brim.

"Don't you worry, my Indian friend. We'll get you there."

The leading news story on channel five was a pack of coyotes negotiating the rough terrain of the San Gabriel Mountains. Felix's mother, Anita, mentioned the irony of *coyotes* eating Mexicans.

"Been doing it for years, one way or another," she said. The coyotes' bodies were lean. They darted in ninety-degree angles like a school of fish, or how you might expect UFOs to move across the sky over Griffith Park on a stony night. Felix thought they ran proudly. He wanted friends like that, a pack he could run with. Felix couldn't relate to the kids he grew up with in the old Pico Rivera neighborhood anymore, with all their light-speed Spanish chatter, and the spider web–tattooed elbows they used to snatch up unsuspecting güeras from the valley.

Anita locked the front door and made her way to the couch. She wrapped her shoulders with a quilt and dug her toes into the seams of the cushions. "Was your grandfather a handful this morning?"

"Ray was fine. He talked about taking his car out for a ride."

"Well, he'd skip outta town if we let him. Probably kill ten people before he got a mile away. The man can't even stand in a shower or pee straight, let alone take care of himself behind the wheel. Felix, it wouldn't surprise me a bit if he were gone one morning. Mijo, he thinks he's indestructible."

"I don't know what to tell you, Mom. If you ask him, he's a man who's got nothing to lose." All the local news coverage had stock footage of coyotes, a constant looping of National Geographic and Discovery splices: coyote heads poking out from underground, carrying small rodents across plains in a gallop, and paranoid in their movements, unlike the Sierra Madre coyotes that roamed like eastside gangs down in the L.A. basin, chests puffed out—vato dogs.

Anita extended her legs across Felix's lap. "He's an outlaw."

"Maybe." Felix nodded. "His mind is getting worse, though. He doesn't take his medication like he should."

Ray walked into the living room right out of the shower, patches of soap stuck to his side, an archipelago of Mr. Bubble on his mottled skin. His chest wall had a recessed cavity between his nipples that looked as though he had been hit with a carnival mallet. He turned to Felix and slapped himself across his naked flanks. "Still bleeds when I piss, Sequoyah."

Anita shook her head, leaned in close to Felix. "Ray still thinks you're an Indian?"

"No, Ray thinks I am *the* Indian."

The real Sequoyah died in 1843 while traveling to Mexico to find a group of Cherokee that had migrated south into Mexico after the Trail of Tears. Felix read that his gravesite has never been found and that it is supposed to be on Texas-Mexico border, in Coahuila. Sequoyah didn't seem like much of a warrior to Felix, not like the image he had in his head as to how Indians ought to look and behave. For the most part, other Cherokees looked like *Indians*—Felix often thought about his own look, how it did not match with the Mexicans down in the valley, not the immigrants, but the extreme La Razas. He remembered his boys from Pico, and his cousins from Montebello, how when they bent back in their stance, their jerseys splayed out to the sides like insect wings. Stingers cocked. They had straight up told him, *Holmes, you are a minus ten on the Mexican scale, and we don't know what to make of you.*

His family had done its best to extract him from the Mexican he'd been hell bent on becoming. Lengua?! What language? Felix felt like the New Coke of the family, a reformulation of Mexican. The problem was that it did not hide his last name, Pérez. It didn't cover the graffiti on the gray cinder block in the back alley where he grew up, or reattach his cousin's thumb after a fight in that same alley with a puto named Poof. It didn't stop the dancing at quinceañeras or turn piñatas into birthday cakes. Tortillas into Wonder Bread. It didn't keep the Los Angeles Dodgers from getting their collective asses kicked by the New York Yankees in the 1978 World Series, the first year in the new house. Mostly, it didn't stop his father from getting his hair cut twice a week by a huera who slipped a Chanel-smelling love letter into his pocket that Felix's mother eventually found and then dropped to her knees while cleaning stains off his pants. It was the Mexican classic: the Farrah Fawcett–family switcheroo.

No doubt Felix could relate to the full-page lithograph of Sequoyah in the *Encyclopædia Britannica*, and how it didn't look anything like an Indian. Sequoyah wore a red cloth wrapped around his head like a turban. Felix showed Ray. "This guy. Right here. *This* is Sequoyah?"

"Damn straight. Like looking in a mirror!" he responded.

Felix read the caption a second time to be sure this was the Indian Ray insisted he was deep down. There were no feathers in Sequoyah's hair, no war paint on his face. Talk about minus ten on a scale! When Felix thought he should have a harder look, he read the part in Sequoyah's biography about how his father was European, and to Felix, this was the key to Sequoyah's soft heart. Felix wondered how Sequoyah got to have a European father. No way it was accidental love. He read about how Sequoyah and his Cherokee people were part of the Five Civilized Tribes until their membership expired. Did Sequoyah really think he was Indian enough, especially when he looked north to his Choctaw brothers, the Indians who gave the Cherokee their Cherokee name?

Felix had pen pals in Paraguay and Cambodia during his teenage years. It was in response to his mother telling him to get out and meet people his own age. Ray remembering anything at all was a shotgun blast at best, but for some reason, he remembered this about Felix.

"You still writing letters all over the world?"

"No, I stopped that a long time ago," Felix said.

"Did you stop, or did they?" Ray's question felt like a setup.

"I don't remember."

"That means you stopped." Ray slid his hand across the porch railing to take his seat. "If they stopped, you'd have an unfinished feeling in your gut, like you're still waiting on something."

"I never thought about it that way, Ray."

"I never thought about it that way, Ray," he mimicked. "You know, they called those talking leaves."

"Who's *they*, Ray? No, no, let me guess . . ."

Felix organized Ray's silverware, unfolded his napkin, and put it across his lap.

"Cherokee. They called letters talking leaves. You wrote so many damn talking leaves. Sequoyah, goddamn it. You don't gotta invent another language, but for Chrissakes."

Ray slapped the newspaper on the breakfast table and tapped his crooked finger on the front page of the local section—a picture of four children spinning on a merry-go-round, their bodies moving faster than shadows trailing underneath them. It was a picture taken last December at the winter solstice festival. They had knit caps on, and smoky breath. The picture seemed surreal in the middle of July. Felix turned the newspaper around to read the headline. Ray used his butter knife, still married to a glob of margarine, to point at the article. Felix winced as he read, *Dogs Will Hunt.*

Ray went back to bed, so Felix decided to go for a run before it got too hot. He felt a quiet toughness running through the neighborhood. No one to call him out. The trailhead that led into the foothills of the San Gabriel Mountains was marked by a collection of posters stapled to the visitors sign by the Department of Fish and Wildlife, warning of coyotes. Felix heard the rumbling of a vehicle coming up the road to the trailhead. A white Parks and Recreation truck hooked around the bend and pulled into the dirt parking lot. It stopped with its tailgate at the trash cans. A woman with a high-arching ponytail stepped out to check a green trash barrel and the heavy chain that held it in place. Her shirt was one size too big. The sleeve cuffs fell around her hands, and she had to keep pulling them back. Felix nodded to her and wondered if she might come over and warn him about being alone with a coyote warning in full effect. She rummaged through some recyclables, then climbed into her truck and drove away without acknowledging Felix.

There were no other cars in the parking lot. *What if he ran into a pack of coyotes?* Felix conversed with himself about a possible confrontation. He couldn't remember the finer details: *Do you run, or do you play dead? Do you make yourself appear bigger, or do you lie down and curl in a ball? Or is that for bears?* Shit, boy, you gonna have to fight your way out. It seemed like important information to know instinctively. He couldn't outrun one coyote, let alone a whole pack. Felix knew that much. He turned and followed the tire tracks out of the dirt lot and back into the neighborhood to play it safe before heading back to commit to Ray the rest of the day.

The steep route up Auburn Avenue was hell on his lungs. Felix stopped at the end of the block and doubled over to catch his breath. A dog barked and raced out from around the corner house. It was a gray-and-white akita that ran along the fenced yard, gnashing its teeth at Felix. It bloodied its nose against the fence as Felix swallowed the scream that started to creep out. The dog kicked over his water bowl and bowed the fence out from its cemented footings. It took almost a minute of wiping the sweat from his eyes before Felix realized that this was Marisol's house.

A voice boomed from the garage. "Heel!" A woman came out and grabbed the dog by his choke collar. "I hope he didn't scare you." She righted the water bowl and forced the dog to sit at her side.

"No, I'm good. That's why you have him." Felix felt as though he was standing outside a celebrity's house. "I mean, it's his job, right? It's why you got him."

"Not everybody thinks that way. It's not the runners we're trying to keep away."

"Sure." Felix didn't want to hint anything about a mauling. "I get it. It's necessary to . . . you got to——" Before he could finish, a little girl ran off the front porch at full speed. She screamed *mommy*, but it sounded like *muddy*. It was deaf little Marisol. She burst onto the lawn and hid behind her mother's leg, opposite the akita. The dog looked up at the woman, then tilted his head to lick Marisol across the face. Marisol pulled back and winced, then turned her attention up to her mother.

She signed with one hand and slurred something that sounded like, *I need your help inside.* She yanked her mother in the direction of the house. The first thing Felix noticed was the wetness in her voice. He couldn't tell if it was because she was deaf, or because of what the coyotes had taken from her. She wore gloves on her hands that seemed as practical as a pair of socks—the thin white kind that pallbearers and Mickey Mouse wear. Marisol clasped the excess skin on the dog's head with both hands and pulled back. Felix could see the fine capillaries in the dog's eyes.

"Again, sorry if he startled you." The woman let go of the dog and turned her attention to Marisol, who was now out from behind her mother's legs.

"It's not a problem. A lot of people are doing what they can around here to keep the neighborhood safe."

"Are they?" She picked up the water bowl.

"A fence and a dog. That's about all you can do, I suppose."

"It's funny to me that you think people around here are doing what they can." Felix felt the slow press of her verbal foot on his throat. "Going back in time is about the only thing that could help at this point."

The woman walked away, pulling Marisol in tow. Felix caught a glimpse of Marisol's face in the sunlight that cut a pillared shape into the front lawn. She had scarring from under her right eye to just below her chin. Her lips were slightly offset and didn't make a good seal. The *San Gabriel Valley Tribune* had said she would need multiple surgeries to fix the damage done by the coyotes, that she might never look the same again. Felix had expected worse. She pulled away and twirled in and out of the sunlight in tight circles around her mother. Felix didn't know what she looked like before the attack, but here she looked and acted like any little girl. Felix turned to start up the hill. He tightened his laces and finished the conversation: "At the end of the day, she's a lucky girl." It did not matter how Felix meant the words, but he might as well have come out and said, *You are a dumbass puta for not being a better mother. Look what you did to your own daughter.*

"Who the fuck do you think you are?" It seemed like an easy question, and one he'd been getting a lot lately. He abandoned his untied shoe. "Are you from around here?" The woman shook her head. "I wrapped parts of my daughter's face in a towel. She couldn't sign to me what she needed because the palms of her hands were practically eaten away. They were hamburger. Tell me, what exactly do you tell a deaf girl to do as she shows you her hamburger hands over and over to you like *you* are blind? What do you think of that?" Felix thought about Marisol's screaming and wondered if she could hear herself inside her head, or was it just an indecipherable vibration? The woman threw the water bowl at the fence. "Don't ever come here with that kind of bullshit optimism again."

The dog loped back across the yard and forced his nose through a square of chain link. His chest expanded with Felix's scent; he exhaled and snorted saliva across Felix's shins before following Marisol and her mother inside the house.

Felix read aloud to Ray a quote from a man named Jack Kilpatrick, an ethnographer who had spent much of his life studying superstar Indian Sequoyah: *Sequoyah was always in the wilderness. He walked about, but he was never a hunter. I wonder what he was looking for.* Ray's face turned red and flexed what muscles he had left in his body. "Looking for the goddamned recipe on how to be the goddamnedest Indian ever made. Its not rocket math, boy."

Felix scratched his head. "It sounds like most people thought that, at the end of the day, he didn't do shit, Ray. Language or no language, he's somewhere in an unmarked and unclaimed grave."

"No matter. Sequoyah, you got yourself an empty gut, and I don't know what to make of it."

Felix opened Ray's medication. He tapped the powder from the capsules into Ray's soup. He wasn't even sure the medication was doing anything for Ray, as much as he had been missing the doses that were now either being spit into the garden or fed to the cat.

Anita walked into the kitchen. "What's all the yelling about?"

"Sequoyah here has got a raw gut," said Ray.

"Honey, it's easier if you just play along." Anita picked up around Ray, petting his bowed back each time she passed him. "Did you give him his medication?" Felix held up the empty capsules and mouthed from across the room that he had sabotaged Ray's meal.

"He's a kid again," Anita said. "The two of you are alike that way. But your grandfather is as unpredictable as they come. You— no, you never surprised me with anything the way he does." Ray looked out over the front porch, down to the street. The loss of blood in his face and the drop in his shoulders told Felix that Ray was having an episode. His brain was changing shifts. Ray waved down to two kids on bright orange big wheels spinning donuts in the street. Felix could hear their mother screaming from a second-story window three house over to get their *pinche asses inside, or else.*

Felix tried to catch Ray before he completely fell out. He handed Ray his cowboy hat and bottom dentures, and made eye contact. "I saw her, Ray," Felix said. "Marisol, Ray, the little girl from the coyote attack. I saw her today. She's beautiful." Ray didn't respond as Anita entered the room with a robe in her hand.

"C'mon, Ray, let's get you cleaned up."

Ray smiled widely and reached out to her like a child.

Felix helped out Simon's janitorial business when his mother watched Ray on her days off. It was only a few hours a week, but enough that Felix didn't feel like an animal trapped in his mom's home. The work contract alone made for interesting work. Orion Pictures went bankrupt in the late nineties and sold their remaining worth to Metro-Goldwyn-Mayer. Orion just left all their shit and bailed. Most of the old movie props were sold to auction, or donated to fad restaurants to drive up the price of a BLT. What was left over ended up in rented spaces all over Los Angeles. Major studio property had no storage room for *RoboCop 1, 2,* or *3.*

They had no room for *The Great Santini.*

Simon gave Felix a set of keys, cleaning supplies, and the instructions that even though Hollywood really didn't give a shit anymore about any of this stuff, try not to break anything.

The warehouse was a one-hundred-foot-by-fifty-foot white metal-sided rectangle in Norwalk that had no identifying signage, just a blocked address number over a double-padlocked door. There were no windows. Felix powered on the fluorescent lights that matched the outfield intensity of a night game at Chavez Ravine. He walked the cinematic graveyard, running his feather duster along the row of decommissioned Terminator mannequins in fake black leather. Some had sunglasses with one lens missing. These were the versions used to throw through walls and roll out of semis at high speed. Felix felt inspired by the props to watch movies that he and Ray had never seen. He'd rent *The Silence of the Lambs, The Falcon and the Snowman,* and *Platoon,* paying close attention to items on the sets. Felix pictured himself throwing a no-no in *Bull Durham,* or playing the trumpet at *The Cotton Club.* He'd point out the props hidden in movies that were now decorations in the bathrooms he scrubbed. If Ray was ever impressed, he rarely showed it.

"Tell Ray I am on my way home." Felix kicked his feet up on the desk and made tiny yellow airplanes from Post-Its.

Anita sounded exhausted on the phone. "I will, but it won't have much effect. It's been a bad day for Ray. This afternoon, I thought he was napping. Felix, I found him in the backyard, sitting in the fire pit. And it was an hour before I realized he had a dead bird in his pocket. I'm just saying he might not know who you are today, mijo."

Felix flew a paper airplane from the desk that made tight loops before sticking into the mesh screen on the side of the metal trashcan. "He'll know who I am."

Mrs. Gutiérrez spotted the first pack of coyotes digging in the sand at the Montessori, as though they were uncovering hidden bones. Anita told Felix he'd better be careful getting home, that at this point she didn't even trust the walk up the driveway. Some neighbors had set up rolling phone lists in case of an emergency, to get everyone's pets inside, children rounded up and under their beds! Mrs. Gutiérrez called everyone on her list to update the last sightings. Ella was made for this. For a woman who stayed at home and raised a family alone, with a husband whose body came home from Desert Storm unrecognizable, this was her moment to brand *Gutiérrez* into the hillside with a hot iron. When Anita hung up the phone with her for the third time that evening, she turned to Felix and told him that this señorita was made of that super high-grade new-car steel.

"The soccer fields at Saint Rita's, Felix. That's a block away."

It was also the most direct route between the business center of town and the trailhead.

"She said there were six." And before Felix could ask their direction, Anita turned on the porch light and opened the drapes. "She said they were heading this way."

Ray sat in the corner of the living room. He held his cane up like a gun and looked down its encrusted barrel at the television. "I'll shoot 'em from the porch." Ray swung his cane around and stopped with the drop on Felix. "You there. Help me up."

Anita shut the drapes. "Ray, you are not going outside."

"Woman, you been squabbling at me all day." Ray reached into his pants pocket with a look on his face that said he expected something to be there that wasn't. He waved Felix over to the couch and pulled him down by his shirt pocket to look him in the eye. "Your name?"

"It's me, Felix."

Ray took a moment, flipping his bottom teeth in and out of his mouth with his tongue. It reminded Felix of the hourglass symbol on his computer when he asked it to do too much.

"Well, Felix, you say. Get my old ass outside."

"What do you need out there, Ray?"

"We're only gonna get one shot at this."

Anita shook her head. "He's all yours. I am calling Mrs. Gutiérrez back to get an update."

Felix rolled Ray's sleeves down to cover the tears in his skin that came with a bad day wandering. He lifted Ray to his feet and escorted him to the front of the house. "There's wild dogs outside, and I'm gonna get me a few."

"I can sit out here with you, Ray."

Ray looked Felix over. "No, and hell no. You ain't built this way." Ray sat back on a worn Adirondack and reached out for his cane. "Just hand me my gun." Felix cleaned the cane with the end of a wool blanket that Anita had bought on Olvera Street. He handed it to Ray and spread the blanket down over his legs.

"I'll be back to check on you in a bit."

"Mm." Ray sat intent.

It took three times to turn her over, but Felix could see through the kitchen window that the roar of the Mustang's engine had startled his mother. He got out of the car and unlocked the gate that separated the front and back of the house. Anita tapped on the kitchen window with a ladle. Felix could make out the words on her lips: *You're crazy, LO-CO!* Again and again, pointing at her lips, *LO-CO, LO-CO!* She reached above her head, raising question about the Indian headdress Felix now wore—a feathered ceremonial headdress that fanned out from Felix down along his spine. Each barb was dyed blue with a dipped deep blood red at each tip. Felix rubbed his fingers across his forehead to feel its delicate beadwork that slightly dug into his forehead and then down into long strands that hung loose, framing the straight lines of his jaw. The feathers were the cleanest haircut he'd ever had. He tilted back on his heels like his cousins would in Montebello, nodded up to his mother in the window, and tucked his thumbs under soft hide. He pulled off the tag that slid from the plumage and read it aloud: "Check it, Ma—*Dances with Wolves*, lot twenty-three, item number one dash zero zero three." Felix and Simon had debated at the warehouse after their shift was over about whether the movie was based on the Sioux or the Cherokee.

Felix propped the gate open with the two sun-warped trash cans. The upholstery in Ray's Mustang smelled appropriately like horsehair. Felix settled into the driver's seat as the stitching ripped under his Cherokee weight. The faded leather dashboard was split open around all the gauges. A desert crust. Felix tapped each gauge to see if they had as much play as the steering wheel that he rocked from side to side just to keep the car in a straight line for the twenty-foot stretch. He pulled the Mustang from the side of house and into Ray's view. The Mustang popped and clinked before settling into a purring idle. Felix made sure to slide the transmission into park and double-check the emergency brake. He dusted off the passenger seat. He negotiated the loose hanging visor around the beaded artwork, bent down low so not to pull the feathers from headdress where it peaked ever skyward. He did the three-sixty around the car to check the tires and noticed there wasn't one drop of oil on the concrete pad. The Mustang backfired and sent Felix to the ground. An orchestra of howls harmonized in the direction of Saint Rita's. Felix waved his hand in front of the headlights to check the beam. The headdress had such a wingspan that Felix's shadow darkened the driveway down to the street. Ray bent down to see the man underneath.

"Hot damn, hot damn, if it's not you, Sequoyah."

Felix took Ray's hand and led him to the car. The headdress mesmerized Ray, and Felix made sure to let him know he could touch it. "Go ahead, Ray. It's the real deal. One hundred percent Cherokee."

Ray nodded with his approval. Felix opened the passenger-side door. "Wanna go for a ride?"

The howls continued, and it sounded as though the coyotes were on the move, perhaps even splitting up now, as the echoes bounced through the neighborhood from all directions. Ray straightened up and set his cane inside the car. "We're gettin' us some dogs, right?"

"We'll see what's out there, Grandpa."

Felix turned the Mustang south onto the steep descent of Auburn. They crossed Olive Avenue and West Allegra before turning east on West Montecito. The Mustang ran strong. Felix pressed down on the gas and dropped it into a passing gear, knowing he had the straight. It settled back into a hum and vibration that lulled the two men out of starting any conversation. Under the neon waving cartoon enchilada sign at Taco Fiesta that filled the Mustang with warm red light, they turned north on Grove Lane and headed back toward the foothills in a search grid pattern.

"We got to cover our tracks, Sequoyah."

It was the reflection off the back of six coyotes' eyes, sitting on their haunches and perfectly divided by the double yellow lines that caused Felix to throw the car into neutral and slowly depress the brakes. They sat so beautifully erect that Felix thought this was not a quest for blood and terror. Then they skittered around in tight circles, a primal dance that Felix could not decode under streetlights. They reminded him of his boys back in Pico Rivera, cackling nonsense and disinterested in the world. He wanted to erase that image in his head. Reinvent him some Indian. He revved the engine and thought about Sequoyah—how Sequoyah wandered the desert, searching but never a hunter, that maybe his grave was unmarked because there was no such grave. That maybe Sequoyah ended up nothing more than food for wild dogs on a path to an old world he knew nothing about.

Felix shifted into drive. The click of the transmission sounded like the loading of a rifle's chamber. Ray lifted his cane to the dash and pressed its curved end into his hollow shoulder. Felix pulled the nylon webbing on Ray's seat belt until it cinched down snug. He straightened the feathers on the headdress over the center console and adjusted the rearview mirror. He imagined every house on the block to be little Marisol's house. Ray leaned over and poked his finger into Felix's ribs. He told Felix that he better not miss a one.

LAS PALMAS BALLROOM

Alma lay next to her son Robert in his bed to see the yard as he did. His view included a large mound of dirt that grew steadily throughout the summer, her heavily dented Chevy Malibu in the driveway, and the bus stop for the elementary school. There was not much movement in Robert's day except early in the morning when the kids gathered and called each other shitheads. They'd sometimes fight in the late afternoons. She imagined Robert sliding on the loosened gravel and fighting with the Hernandez brothers. Bruising from a punch and not the pressure sores his thirty-year-old body endured from simply lying in one spot for too long.

Alma heard Carl's boot heels tapping on the metal screen door. "Prima, where are you?"

"We're in the back room." Alma sat up and finished washing Robert's hair over an empty basin in the bedroom. "I am cleaning Roberto." She covered her son with a dry towel and removed the tape that covered his tracheotomy, which caused him to spasm.

Alma waved Carl away as he walked into the room. "Back up so I can put Robert back on his vent."

Carl lifted Robert into his wheelchair. Alma opened a sterile package with new tracheotomy hardware inside. Her hands were damp, and it made it difficult to pull the gloves around her bony fingers. She applied lubricant to the breathing tube's tip and tilted its end ninety degrees into the hole in Robert's neck, then twisted downward into position, always careful to avoid the ribbed cartilage the nurse had told Alma she could poke right through if she wasn't careful. That she would certainly know if she had.

"Cough, mijo." Alma lifted her finger off the catheter that activated the suction. "Again." Robert coughed again. A collection of clear phlegm lined the basin, which pleased Alma. She detached the suction unit and wiped the rounded opening that the nurse had called the obturator. She secured the tube with the inflated cuff at its end, which caused Robert to pull back. The Velcro neck strap was worn and took Alma several tries to get the two ends to stick together behind his neck. And with the same ease as the flip in her tortillas, she attached Robert to his ventilator.

Carl watched from across the room. "You can do that in the dark, Alma."

"I've been taking care of a sick boy too long."

"I'll be in the kitchen. There's something I've been wanting to show you."

"Pour some coffee." Alma looked to the floor at the pea gravel Carl had stamped out on the carpet. "And clean all that up." Alma gathered the used breathing tube, the suction, and guide wires, and placed them in a red bag the size of a pillowcase marked *Biohazard*. The black horned symbol on its side resembled the devil. She winced every time she opened its end. She took off the sterile gloves and blew away the fine baby powder from the creases in her palms. Alma exercised Robert's arms and legs, measuring his range and the amount of lost muscle. She placed hand towels between his arms and the leather armrests, so that his paper-white skin wouldn't burn from the direct sunlight that filtered through the large bay windows.

Carl sat at the breakfast table with a duffel bag opened at his feet. A stack of magazines lined up neatly between the table's edge and his coffee, partially covered by his Brooklyn Dodgers cap, which had a large *B* stamped at its center. Alma reached across the place mat to pick it up off the table. "More comics. I told you, Carl, he's not a boy."

Carl grabbed Alma's wrist. "Stop."

"I've told you that Robert doesn't need to read those anymore."

"These aren't comics, prima, and you better take a deep breath." Carl turned the top magazine so that Alma could read the title. "I cleaned my garage last week and found these. I think they'd do Robert some good."

Alma read *Playboy* across the top. She recognized the woman on the cover from the movies. She wore a black cowboy hat and had a cigar in her mouth; a camisole and suspenders pushed her breasts together. Alma pulled her sweater tight around her own breasts and read aloud the caption: "*Bo Derek, X-rated—She's Hotter Than Ever*. . . . What is this business?"

Carl didn't give her a chance to finish. "Even you said he's not a boy anymore."

She spread out the other magazines on the table. "Why would you do this, Carl?"

"These are for Robert. It's time he sees these things, Alma." Carl reached into his duffel bag. "He's not going to get the chance—"

"To what, Carl?" She turned the magazine over, which only revealed a half-naked woman on the back cover, blowing kisses across a snifter of cognac.

"To be with a woman. He should know what it's like," said Carl.

"Listen to what you're saying! You can't decide that for him."

Alma pulled her shaking hands away twice before Carl could take hold again. "He's a thirty-year-old man, period, end of discussion. We have to think about him as a man."

"And what do you expect *these* are going to do for him?"

"I think he'll know when he sees them. I did. It's the same thing as the comics that way. We're taking the boy to the man."

Alma rolled her eyes.

He slid the stack onto her place mat. "They'll take him somewhere he's never been. I can't imagine never touching a woman." Carl pushed his chair away from the table and stood, pointing at the crucifix on the far kitchen wall between two copper pots. "Nuestro Padre, thank you for blessing me with all the beautiful women that've come into my life." He pointed down to Alma. "Please help this very old and narrow-sighted woman understand."

Alma smacked him. "As many women as you've touched, Carl, I'm not giving Bo Derek to Robert. She can go be *Hotter Than Ever* back in your garage."

Carl opened to Bo's centerfold. "You can't deny it, Alma. Your boy has his father Oscar in him somewhere, just itching to get out." He smeared his finger across Bo Derek's abdomen, as if to wipe away the small droplets of sweat pooling in her belly button. "You should watch him like I do when he sleeps, so you can see that there are things happening in Robert's dreams he can't explain to us."

"That's the muscular dystrophy, not his father's ways." Alma turned away and wiped her eyes. She walked out to where Robert sat with his face full of sun, his head slightly tilted back against the headrest as if lounging on a beach. His fingers contracted and then released. It upset Alma that his movements reminded her of a robot. She turned back to Carl. "I don't even know what to do with him as a man."

"I know a place we can take him," Carl said. "He can dance with a woman for the first time. No harm in that, prima."

Alma had met Oscar at the shipyard back home in Long Beach, where he'd worked as a commercial diver with Carl. She fell in love with him after only seeing his eyes behind the thick Plexiglas shield of his yellow dive helmet. He wore gloves that seemed useless for even opening a door, let alone doing the precise welding he did in deep water, water described in fathoms, and she had wondered how it might feel to have his gloved hands under her shirt, clumsily traversing her. She wasn't the only girl who ever came to the shipyard. It was the place to find a man that could provide. On occasion, Alma recognized some of the girls from her Pico Rivera neighborhood, older girls with their scribbled-on eyebrows and red lipstick. Even at seventeen, she wasn't allowed to wear anything other than colorless gloss from Newberry's. And when she had tried to sneak out of the house with a lip color named Crimson Desire, it became evident that her mother *did* know everyone in Los Angeles.

To get ahead of the pack, she finally told Oscar after a month of flirting and bringing him lunches that he'd better start thinking about asking her out on a full-time basis. Their first date was to Philippe's for French dips. Oscar used the sawdust on the floor to describe shield-metal and flux-cored arcs, letting the dust fall from his fingertips to make pictures on the graffitied countertops. She wore a leopard-print sundress that she had hemmed two inches above her knee the day she bought it. Oscar went on at length about friction when he first held her hand, and how when he was underwater too long, he could taste the metal in his mouth.

"It's the alloy of mercury in your fillings," he'd said. "They call it dental amalgam."

Alma shook her head at his words.

Oscar had opened his mouth and pointed to the silver caps that covered five of his top teeth, six on the bottom. He slobbered. "I can taste the fillings in my mouth when the electricity really gets goin'." He slid his left hand up and along Alma's thigh. She didn't mind. Opening his mouth, he took Alma's longest finger and ran its tip along two silver-capped molars. They felt like turquoise Indian jewelry to Alma. Oscar convulsed with fake electricity that surged through his body, and gnawed on Alma's finger down to her knuckle. She laughed out loud and pulled her finger away, then pressed her leg closer to his. She thought about the time she had accidently chewed on a tinfoil wrapper, how when she bit down, it was more color than flavor in the back of her mouth.

You could do all you could imagine, and it still wasn't enough for Alma to get Oscar to be a one-woman man. She was never surprised by the smell of women on his fingers. She'd tell herself while under the weight of his body at night that she deserved better, that given some serious thought, she might consider never seeing him again. And when she became pregnant with Robert, it rearranged all the thoughts in her head as to finding a new man. Damn it, she should. A new man would be like winning the showcase on *The Price Is Right*. She pictured that flirty gringo Bob Barker handing her the keys to the fancy new car that she would drive to her new life. Oh, the kiss she'd plant on him!

When Alma went to tell Oscar that she was having his baby, he had just finished a two-day pipe-welding job at Dos Cuadras Offshore Oil Field in the Santa Barbara Channel and was forced to spend seventy-two hours in the hyperbaric chamber. Alma peeked through the window. She had written *baby* on the dive company's letterhead, accompanied with a crude cartoon drawing of the inside of her belly. She tapped on the glass and Scotch-taped the note inside the small metal window frame of the chamber. She never lifted it to see his reaction.

That night Alma dreamt of Bo Derek. Her big black hat and cigar deep in her mouth. She dreamt of the two of them sitting in Alma's rusted Malibu in the driveway, looking at photo albums. She showed Bo Derek a picture of Oscar in his wet suit pulled down around his waist from when they first started dating. Water beaded on his hairy chest as he looked at the end of an ignited welding torch. Bo Derek approved. She's been with her lion's share of men, Alma thought. Alma asked if she could touch the supermodel's skin, which looked as soft as the underside of the leaves in her tomato garden. Bo didn't mind, even pointing out the softest spots on her wrist and behind her knee. As she turned the pages, she noticed that Bo Derek had replaced her in every photo—Oscar is feeding Bo Derek in this snapshot, and he is kissing her neck in another. Here is the supermodel and movie star Bo Derek nursing a half-sleeping Robert the day he was born. Page after page, every photo of Alma was replaced with Bo Derek. Even if Alma had remembered herself in the background of this photo, hidden away in the kitchen checking the temperature of the posole at Christmas, the dream chose Bo Derek to blow across the soup and wince at the abundance of freshly crushed oregano steeping its broth.

   Alma woke. She climbed out of bed and walked down the hall to check on Robert. The lights coming from the Albertsons parking lot filled his room with a milky glow. His tremor medication often took time before it kicked in and slowed the jerking in his muscles, so Alma always checked on him when she woke during the night to pee. It was something that his doctors said he'd eventually get used to, but he never did. Robert's hand rested on the three-legged metal end table that Oscar had welded for Alma from broken ocean pipe. He had given it to her the day they moved into their first apartment. *It's a triangle*, he had said, the strongest shape known to man. But now, watching the twitch in her son, Alma wished that Oscar hadn't been such a good welder, and that the table would just break apart in the night like the water pipes in the crawl space had every few years, then maybe she'd finally be able to throw it away. But whom was she kidding—no way she could even drag it to the curb on trash day!

   She whispered to Robert as he slept. "Mijo, if you want to dance with a girl, squeeze my finger twice." There was nothing. "Mijo. Squeeze once if I sound ridiculous." Robert squeezed Alma's finger twice and then wouldn't let go. He squeezed so hard that Alma thought he might be having a seizure. Robert's doctor had described how his body might act when seizing, that it was just part of all the goodies that came with a basketful of disease, and how she should prepare for the inevitable because it was an *any moment* sort of deal. He had used the word *dystonic* in his medical offices in Montebello, and Alma had just smiled and nodded politely when he continued on about diaphoretic presentation and a possible, and very likely, apneic and postictal period, which was much like a computer rebooting after a hard shutdown.

Robert's first seizure had been in the corner booth at Rafael's after Ash Wednesday Mass. And at that moment, at light speed, Alma knew exactly what all the terms had meant—the full-body shaking, the profuse sweating, and the breathlessness. Robert had turned blue, and the busboys couldn't find enough towels to dry his body; the palm ash cross on his forehead washed away like glacial silt. Then the urine. The waitress brought extra napkins and a small trash can for someone, anyone, to throw up into. She brought an ice-cold 7Up, then sat down in the booth where Alma had been sitting, and not knowing what more to do, she just apologized over and over again about the breakfast order taking so long.

"This one, Carl." Alma held up a white dress shirt she had worn during a catering job the previous spring at Echo Park. "There's a stain right here, but I think a nice tie would cover it up just fine." She licked her thumb and scrubbed the discolored trim along the buttons. The taste of her own stain was awful.

"I don't think you should put him in girl clothes," Carl said.

"This is for both men and women. They call it unisex."

"Did you wear it?" Carl asked.

"You listen like a rock. I told you—last spring, Carlito."

"Then, prima, this is a girl shirt. There's no way around that. Let me go to my truck. I have something behind my seat we can iron."

Carl came back holding a yellow short-sleeved guayabera. Its seams ran the length of the shirt with embroidered birds-of-paradise at the edges of all four pockets. A real beauty!

"Flores, Carl. How is that better than my shirt?" Alma folded the shirt over and inspected the stitching. It was fine work.

"The Legend." Carl raised his fist into the air.

"Qué dices, the legend?" Alma asked.

"The shirt. It's called the Legend. Mira the tag." Carl took the shirt from Alma and flipped over the collar. He held it up to Alma, pinching the shirt together at the shoulders. The light cut through and exposed all the delicate stitching. "The chica who takes this shirt off Roberto will want to keep it forever."

"You said dancing," said Alma.

"You'll see, La Leyenda—that is what they will call him." Carl laid the shirt across Robert's chest. "That is what they will call you, mijo." He turned to Alma. "And you, old woman, you should know that you will never find a better listener than a rock."

Alma prayed the rosary from Atlantic Boulevard to Century Boulevard. It wasn't a long drive with Carl behind the wheel, but she managed to get deep into the fourth sorrowful mystery—*Taking My Son to a Dancing Prostitute*. She imagined all the turns in her life that eventually led her to a club called Las Palmas Ballroom, which from the curb looked like nothing more than a normal ranch home much like her own, with a glowing red bulb under the awning.

Alma leaned into Carl's good ear. "Are you sure this—"

"I've been here before. It will be okay."

Alma shook her head at Carl's reassurance. "You lower Robert down while I get my things together."

Carl opened the van's sliding door. Robert woke and smiled at him. "Let's go, mijo." Carl imitated the noise the van's hydraulic lift made as Robert's chair settled to the street, crunching a plastic water bottle under its weight, sending its white cap skipping across the sidewalk into a patch of ice plant. Alma stood at the base of four shallow stairs that led up to the entrance.

"Go and park around the corner, Carlito."

"It's dark. Who's gonna care about nothing?"

Alma put her coin purse into the emergency-kit pouch that slung over Robert's chair. "And stay with the van in case we have to leave in a hurry."

"You're talking like we're robbing a bank," said Carl.

"After doing all this, I know robbing a bank would be easier," said Alma.

She used her embroidered handkerchief to clean the smudges from the silver plate marked *Doorbell* before depressing its yellowing button. Carl idled toward the corner around the house into the alley. Music from inside vibrated concentric circles in the puddles on the sidewalk. Alma looked through the missing edges of window tinting that stretched across the front windows. Red lights warmed the space inside. She wondered why it was taking so long and rang the bell again. She stepped back and waited by Robert in his wheelchair as the door opened, revealing a full-bodied woman in a cascading blue sequin dress that swung down from her arms. Her voice twanged. "Can I help you, darling?"

Alma peeked inside past the woman to the flock of white cowboy hats on the dance floor in the middle of the room. Alma moved Robert's wheelchair forward. The left wheel spun freely under the chair until it clasped on to the gravel, thrusting him to the edge of the porch.

"Do you have a ramp?" The woman gave a confused look. Alma wondered if she had a problem understanding her broken English. Alma made a shape that resembled a ramp with her left hand, and then used her fingers to walk up its slant. "Please—do you have—a ramp for wheelchairs?"

"No, I'm sorry, we don't." Alma felt a great distrust from the woman. "Do you need to make a phone call, or get a ride? I can help you with that much." The woman stepped out to get a better look at Robert. Pollen from the trees above dusted him lightly. "Is that boy okay?"

Alma pulled an old grocery receipt from her pocket and unfolded it to reveal the address handwritten on the back. She adjusted her glasses and lifted the receipt above her shoulder so the woman could see from her position at the top of the stairs. "Las Palmas Ballroom?"

"Yes, but why . . . honey, do you know what kind of business Las Palmas Ballroom is?" She stepped down to Alma and Robert and pulled the blue sequin dress into her body so as not to step directly on it or drag it across the porch. The dress reminded Alma of the costumes rodeo clowns wore. Oscar had taken Alma and Robert to Victorville on weekends to the rodeo, back when Robert could still holler at the cowboys clutching hair on the high arcs of the kicking mares. The clowns popped from large barrels like toys and ran down the unpiloted bulls. They shot water cannons at spectators. It was a dress Alma couldn't picture herself wearing.

"My cousin Carl told me there'd be women to dance with here." Alma folded the paper back into a tight square into her pocket. "This is true, no?"

"No, I mean yes. Yes," the woman answered.

Alma blew her nose into the handkerchief. "Bueno. Can you help to get him up the stairs? His chair weighs two hundred pounds." She held up two fingers to the woman. "Two."

The woman nodded and looked back into the glow of the house. "My name is Gloria. I run the place with my son. I know that sounds odd, but you know what they say about beggars." Alma pretended to understand. The women shook hands. Alma wiped the spit forming off the right corner of Robert's mouth. She wanted to make him as presentable as possible.

"Is this your son?" asked Gloria.

"Sí."

"You're his mother?"

The phrase *two birds with one stone* came to Alma's mind in a way that she finally understood, and it seemed like a trick question. "Sí, this is my son, Robert. I am his mother. He is here to see *you*."

"He's not here to see me, darling, but we'll get this sorted out. I make a good business knowing that there's someone for everyone. But I have to tell you, in all my years of doing this, I don't think a mother has ever brought her own flesh and blood to *meet* a girl at Las Palmas Ballroom." Alma smiled and straightened the seam of Robert's shirt. The woman winked. "Let's go inside. I know I have the perfect girl."

Alma gave her hand again to Gloria. "My name is Alma Lopez."

"Well, Alma Lopez, let's get the business stuff out of the way." Gloria stepped back inside and called out to the rhinoceros-sized man who worked as the bouncer. His belly swung like a bag of pinto beans, and his thick arms stretched out the elastic of his shirtsleeves. "This is my son, Anthony." He didn't say a word to Alma but gave her a quiet nod as he pulled a banquet table through the entryway with one hand. Alma felt her jealousy at the strength of Gloria's son warm her body. He fit the table like a puzzle piece to match the angle of the stairs, and placed two large cinder blocks at the top and bottom to keep it from sliding under weight.

Alma showed him how all the controls worked on Robert's chair, moving the lever side to side. Robert rotated smoothly left, then right. Anthony's large fingers dwarfed Robert's clawlike hand. Alma felt a rocket ship blast off in her chest as Anthony took the controls. He thrust Robert's chair over the first plywood edge, which stretched out his coiled ventilator hose. Anthony stopped to reassess and to make sure that he hadn't upset Alma.

Gloria looked down to the street corner. "He with you?" Gloria pointed at Carl peeking through a wood fence.

"Sí, that is my cousin."

Gloria called to Carl, "We could use a little help here, peekaboo."

Robert's tubes pulled so tight that his head sat fixed in a sniffing position against the headrest.

"They're for his breathing," Alma said, pointing to the tubes and filling her own lungs deeply to make her point.

Anthony told Carl to take over the controls. They both squatted low to the ground and leaned into the chair from behind. Alma adjusted Robert in his seat. She fought his natural lean to the right and held him in place as the chair crept forward over the bowing plywood. She wiped more spit away. Anthony kept his feet firmly on the ground as Carl did his best to stay light on his. They pushed the chair up the makeshift ramp until it leveled out on the porch. Alma squeezed Anthony's arm and patted her chest above her heart. "That's how I imagined it," she said.

The lighting effects from the disco ball in the middle of the dance floor played tricks on Alma's eyes as Gloria called her to the counter. "It's twenty-five dollars each for the cover." Gloria stabbed a piece of paper on a long spindle and reached for Alma's hand. She turned over Alma's wrist and stamped it with purple ink that glowed under the black light.

Alma showed Carl how the stamp caught the light, delighted. "I expected it to cost so much more."

"Darling, now you pay by the minute," said Gloria.

The base coming from the large stack of speakers suspended above the dance floor made it difficult for Alma to hear. "Every minute we have to pay you?"

"Every minute you have to pay *for*. You can buy an hour of dances right now. We finish that, and I will take you to find the perfect little gem for your son."

Alma kept her billfold in her purse as she counted her money. She looked to Carl. "Did you know about this?"

"Of course I knew about this. You didn't think it was cheap?"

"How would I know? I don't go dancing with sucias."

Anthony searched Robert's wheelchair, which made Alma visibly uncomfortable.

"We search everyone." Gloria explained the policy in a way that a mother might understand. She stamped Robert's wrist. "He's no different."

Alma appreciated Gloria's sense of motherliness. She put fifty dollars in ones and fives on the counter and straightened all the bills to face the same direction. Carl stepped up and pushed her money aside. He slid Gloria a hundred-dollar bill across the counter like it was something he had been practicing all day in the mirror. "When this runs out," he told her, "you come get me." He struck his chest and nodded a fierce nod.

Each girl wore a small piece of paper pinned to her shirt with a number written in black marker. Gloria lined up the girls who were not dancing along the snack bar. Two girls huddled by themselves near the hot dog cooker to warm themselves under the orange light. The cooker's spinning rollers screeched with each rotation. The girls laughed and pointed at a man sitting against the pillar by the DJ booth, which only prompted him to comb his hair and walk over until they turned him away. Gloria snapped her fingers at the DJ to turn down the music this much. She pulled the tallest girl aside. "Yolanda! You are supposed to be training Lola, not being all best friends on my dime." Yolanda pulled up her skirt to adjust her thigh-high stockings rocking two red bows at the top like cinnamon candy. Fat bulged over the elastic band. Alma shook her head at Carl, who showed an obvious interest. Yolanda leaned back in her red patent heels and gave a hard look to Gloria as she excused herself to use the bathroom.

"I have to pee. Be gone a bit," Yolanda said.

Lola muttered something under her breath about cripples to the other girls and disappeared behind Yolanda into the room's pulsing light.

Each dancer inspected her shoes so as not to make eye contact with Alma, tipping their ankles sideways to look at the bottoms of their soles, as though they had stepped in something in the back parking lot during their last smoke break. They brushed confetti from their dresses from some past event.

"Opal. Where's Opal?" Gloria asked. She yelled to Anthony behind the podium by the entrance. "Find Opal and bring her here. I don't care if she's already dancing."

Before the girls walked away, Alma thanked each one as though she knew them their whole lives. She took their hands into hers and made the sign of the cross over each one. Carl kept a predatory distance. Alma tried twice to get his attention. It wasn't until the music changed that Carl finally looked over. She turned Robert's chair around and lined him up against the wall where Gloria said she should wait. The couples on the dance floor were a mismatch of young girls and older Mexican men that reminded Alma of Oscar.

They pressed their hips into the girls, and smiled as if they were handing out treats. She knew Carl was one of these men. Some of the girls pulled away or kept a distance until they remembered what they were there to do, and then settled back in. Alma dipped her handkerchief into a glass of ice water to wet Robert's dry lips. She straightened his shirt over his bloated stomach.

"Mijo, this will be over soon."

Gloria waited a few feet away with a young girl Alma did not recognize.

"Alma Lopez, this is Opal," Gloria said, presenting the girl as though she were a new car in the showroom, one hand following the length of her body's lines. Opal was not the girl Alma had imagined for Robert. Alma thought about the Indians from deep in Oaxaca. Nothing like the Bo Derek she had dreamt into her photo albums. Opal was obviously the girl who danced with the ugly and crippled men. Alma thought about the family of rats that must've lived in the nest that was Opal's hair. She ran her fingers through her own hair before deciding whether or not to say anything to Gloria. The forehead on this girl! Carl winced from across the dance floor. Alma didn't know the name of the creature that lived under the bridges in Robert's children's books, but in her head, it was Opal, catching children for her dinner and leaving the bones for drunk men to tell tales. Alma suddenly wanted Yolanda. She wanted the girls in the pages of Carl's magazines to come to life and spin across the dance floor in chorus line for her to choose from.

"See, I always have the perfect girl," Gloria said. "I've been doing this a long time."

Alma didn't want to be rude to Opal. It wasn't as if Robert was going to make a family with her. Such feo grandchildren!

"He's better dressed than most here," said Opal.

"His name is Robert."

"Miss Gloria told me 'bout him. Said he's probably never been with a woman. That true?"

Alma nodded.

"What do you want me to do for him?"

Alma pointed to the girls swirling across the room.

"Those girls don't do the extra things. They make good money dancing, but..." She slid a finger along Robert's collar and rubbed its corner between her fingertips. "I like your shirt, Robert." Robert's eyes followed her hands. This was the first time such an exchange had taken place. Alma stepped back to take it in fully, as one might the Grand Canyon or the Eiffel Tower or the shuttle launch.

"Miss Gloria will only let me dance, but I can do more if you want."

This confused Alma. "What more would you do?" she asked.

"I can touch him," said Opal.

Alma needed Carl at that moment to tell her to stop overthinking everything—*let that girl do her pinche job for the boy already!* But Carl was across the dance floor at the far end of the club with Yolanda now, in a green leather booth that could fit ten people. They sat close and stared straight ahead like they were on on a Ferris wheel first date.

Opal assured Alma, "It's dark enough in here to do just about anything."

Alma handed her all the dance tokens and asked if it was enough. Gloria came up behind Opal and put her hands on her waist. They swayed to "El Cantante" playing overhead.

"Don't you agree that Opal is a good pick?" Gloria asked. "Let those kids go do their thing." Gloria acted like they were going to a playground across the street. "Alma Lopez, I'm gonna buy you a drink." Alma explained Robert's chair to Opal. She appreciated Opal's concentration and attention to the finer details, asking simple but important questions on how things worked.

"He'll know what I'm doing then?" asked Opal.

"It's his body that doesn't work so good," Alma explained. She tapped the side of her own head. "But he knows in his head."

"Well, then, I will blow his mind." Opal laughed. "How will I know if he's enjoying it?"

"You'll be able to tell if he isn't," Alma answered.

Gloria and Alma sat side by side on wooden chairs looking out over the dance floor. They didn't talk right away, only gestured to one another that one song was better than another. Opal wheeled Robert across the floor and sat on his lap. She took her right shoe off and rubbed under his pants leg with her bare foot. Such speed, Alma thought.

"Is there a special place reserved for mothers like me?" Alma asked.

"Like what?"

Alma looked around the room. "For mothers who don't know how to raise sons."

"The devil is a busy man," said Gloria. "If the worst thing we've ever done in our lives is allow the ugliest girl in my club to dance with your crippled son, I think we'll go unnoticed. I couldn't make a real good living this long if all this wasn't just about the most important thing in the world. Look at them." She clanked Alma's glass. "Cheers. From one mom to another."

The strobe lights made it difficult for Alma to measure the seriousness on Gloria's face. It sounded scripted, like something she has been trying to convince herself, maybe to help her understand her own son.

"You know that Opal will put her hand down your son's pants. She does it to everyone." Gloria moved her chair closer to Alma's. "He won't be any different. I just don't want you to be surprised. We are mothers. You'd be lying if you told me that's not what you really wanted for him."

Alma sipped her drink. She sat up straight in her chair and looked to Carl, who just then pushed away from Yolanda toward the middle of the booth. Yolanda pulled up on her bra straps and held her fist out to him. She jerked it several times then handed her purse to the new girl as she jumped Carl. He struggled with the weight of Yolanda's doughy body as he threw her onto the floor for knocking two drinks across the table into his lap. Her skirt twisted up around her waist, revealing a boyish pair of underwear. She jolted her head back as Carl threw his remaining tokens in her face, as though she'd just been blasted with buckshot at close range.

Anthony had already sprinted the length of the dance floor by the time Gloria realized what was happening.

"Goddamn pig, Yolanda," Gloria said. Lola crawled on the floor and collected the tokens with the cups of her hands as though she were containing a toxic spill. Anthony reached under the table and grabbed Carl by his ankles, dragging him out from under the booth. The music stopped and all the couples on the dance floor unhinged to catch a glimpse of Carl disappearing under the biggest booth in the club like a drowning man.

So much was happening at once that no one but Alma noticed Opal making her move. Gloria screamed at Yolanda until she could barely breathe, wheezing the words *puta* and *slut* and *fired*. All the excitement stirred up the old confetti on the dance floor. Alma could feel Robert's heart begin to race from across the room in all the spaces of her own.

"Mind your own damn business!" Carl yelled on his way to the exit. He fought Anthony and Gloria out the front door and down to the curb. Some of the men cheered and threw their white cowboy hats into the air like they were attending a bullfight at the Plaza México.

"That's right," Yolanda said, adjusting her skirt. "Treat *me* like that?"

Gloria walked back inside and told the DJ to turn up the music. Carl stood in the middle of the street and offered to fight anyone who might need a lesson. He called out for Yolanda to meet him at the end of the block.

Opal straddled Robert. His bird legs fit between her thighs, his face long lost in the matted perm that swallowed him whole. This made it impossible for Alma to see the exchange between their bodies. She thought about the time she had become pregnant with Robert, the very moment it was biologically certain that he would be. She recalled that it was the same day Oscar had explained the hyperbaric chamber after they had sex. He had been naked on her bed with his arms and legs splayed out wide like tentacles, using his hands to demonstrate the distortion and balance of gasses in his body. Alma had played with him until she again hardened his whole body. And with her ear to his belly, she listened to the churn of his insides as he described the dangerous pull and displacement of nitrogen, how it would just rip you apart from the inside.

CROP DUSTER PLAY SET

The box reads *Crop Duster Play Set*. Inside is a banana-yellow plastic plane that resembles a cake topper. A framing nail runs straight through the cockpit and acts as a handle, the plane's rudder, to keep it in flight between my fingertips. The hangar is blue aluminum with a smiling family of white faces painted on its side—the mother wears a string of pearls and tucks a small black handbag into her chest. The father is in a three-piece suit, wrangling an eager boy on his shoulders, awaiting flight. The two plastic wind socks on the rooftop promise winds that will forever blow from the southwest.

"You always take off into the wind," I say to Luna. "If you don't, it'll somersault you as soon as you pull your nose off the ground."

The Crop Duster Play Set includes three sections of white picket fencing and six plastic figurines wrapped in a wax paper pouch. I take them out one by one and line them up in the deep shag carpet.

"Describe them to me, David," Luna says, her milky-white eyes looking skyward. She's only ever been blind. And they call me the leg-braced cripple from Pico. C'mon.

"They're wearing the same overalls you have on."

"Really?" she asks.

"Carbon copy," I tell her.

Three of the figures hold pitchforks into the air with their mouths wide open, no doubt singing "Aquellos Ojos Verdes" at the tops of their lungs. The other figures are the bean pickers, bent in half at the waist with only the tops of their white cowboy hats showing, lima bean bushels slung over their shoulders like long-haul donkeys.

"Even Mexican toys have broken backs!" I say. And as soon as I finish lining up each figure, Luna reaches out for her half, knocking them all over. She finds one of the bean pickers and traces her finger along its humped back, whispers, *What village are you from—Santa Rosalía, Chihuahua? I know you from somewhere.*

We don't say anything out loud, but I know we both imagine our father's face under each hat brim. I have always wondered what he looks like in Luna's head, if his moustache sits the same way on his lip, and if she can even picture the birthmark covering his right eye, the one that earned him the nickname El Pirata in our family. Luna mimics his talk in the fields. "Pick the lima beans too big, mija, and they'll taste like candle wax. You like to eat candle wax, mijita?" She makes her sour face at the plastic figure. Secretly, we'd eat candle wax every meal if we could. "*This* is the correct size," she says. "Look it." Luna moves the pretend lima beans around in her palm like shiny gold coins pulled from the sea. She holds up the largest one, and the sunlight through the bay window casts shadows on its wrinkled make-believe skin.

"Did you hear that?" I ask.

"No, what?" She closes her eyes to hear better.

"Does that help you?" I ask, tapping her clamshelled eyelids. "When you do that?"

"Sometimes," she says. Her right eye flutters lightly, half-milk-open, measuring the room as whiskers might.

I buzz the yellow plane by her head at an angle she won't hear, and tangle its propeller into her hair like grasshopper legs in June. "Crop dusters come out of nowhere," I say. "You can watch the sky all you want, but you won't see a damn thing. It's all sound." It takes a minute to get the plane free from her black curls that just spring back into place like machined parts made specifically for her head.

"How do you know?" she asks. "You've never seen one before."

"I'll show you," I huff.

The orange carpet flattens easily into a square with my forearm. I run my fingers in the opposite direction of the matted shag to make dark rows that resemble mounds of soft dirt—bean dirt. I snap the fence pieces together and place them at ninety degrees at the edge of the make-believe field.

"Let me be the plane," she says.

"A blind girl can't be the plane," I say. "You'd kill everyone in the room."

The hangar sits at the center so that the painty-smiley family can front-row the action about to take place. I line up the workers—picker-fork-picker-fork-picker-fork—down the longest row, sure to turn their faces away so they don't see any of it coming. And Luna is right. I close my eyes and can hear their collective work-song hum, all the plastic men and their wet click-clack cuts through bean pods.

"Go ahead, Luna," I say. "Feel around."

Luna thrusts forward.

"Your quiet hands," I say.

She touches each plastic worker by name and moves with precision between the rows of dirt without even knowing where each starts and stops. The plane is tucked away behind my back, and the inside of my palm itches like Christmas morning. "I can't see a thing," she says, as the sudden air brakes from a curbside trash truck ratchets down the skin on our drumming hearts.

THE HEALING CAVES OF MARRANO BEACH

Isabel puked violently into a grocery bag. The Saint Jude Hands of Healing Caves brochure clearly stated that vomiting could be a real possibility, and that if it did happen, to consult a physician immediately. Isabel never did anything immediately. That is probably why we are here in the first place. The brochure also warned of redness to the more sensitive skin areas—the armpits and groin, the places where the body absorbs things easily. It warned of headaches and hair loss, but these were the things Isabel had been living with for a year now. Woman Cancer. In small print, the brochure warned of death. Not sudden death, but the possible and eventual kind, which seemed like a calculated risk inside her now-balding head, that patchwork of hair combed flat against her scalp, with a small plastic hibiscus clipped on the left side. When Saint Jude's Hands of Healing Caves weren't causing terrible sickness to Isabel, they did something else, something Isabel had described as wholly scientific—they healed.

The Saint Jude Hands of Healing Caves were discovered last year when the San Gabriel River bank opened up and all that miserably shit-filled water just swirled away into oblivion, leaving nothing but muddy banks and a cave system big enough to drive a Greyhound bus through. Eons of bathwater emptied down the drain. Those who witnessed it said that the pull of the river water around their ankles was stronger than an ocean's back out to sea. They insisted aliens. They insisted sacred Mayan cenotes.

This part of the river was called Marrano Beach and considered a reserve, a protected oasis that was home to some of the rarest and most beautiful birds known to East Los Angeles—that was to say that the land was relatively worthless and boggy and overgrown and really only suitable for some of the poorest families to enjoy on a Saturday afternoon. But it was our oasis. The younger generations called it Pig Beach. If you looked out the passenger-side window of my father's truck on the way to my aunt's house, you'd look out over the narrows, down to the Mexican families splayed out under saplings, sunning and swimming in the muck. Some did laundry to crunch time. They came from all over Los Angeles to take in pea gravel sand, thorny-edged paths, a steady run of water, and eddying pools where their babies played in waterlogged diapers, or simply leapt in naked from tire swings. Some shit there. The Catholic girls from Sacred Heart took advantage of the muddy water's zero visibility to skinny-dip on dark weekend nights when the stars and moon were smogged out. The boys? They got all crazy down in that bed.

What left with the water was replaced by the deadly radioactive gas radon. Levels were so high coming from the caves that the cities of Rosemead, El Monte, and Montebello fought as to whose problem it was to mitigate. None wanted the liability or the cost of quarantine and cleanup, at least not for a beach known for its history of floating pig parts from an upriver slaughterhouse. It took a cattleman from Montana by the name of Don Gannon to fix the problem. It so happens that an excessive level of deadly radon gas is a pure money-maker.

Pinche radon.

I cleaned up Isabel, wiping away the sweat from behind her neck.

"I feel better," she said.

"Everyone feels better after throwing up," I said. "It's the release." I pulled her sweat pants up around her beanpole waist and cinched the drawstring that seemed to lengthen from week to week. "But do you feel better-better?"

"Hold my flower." Isabel took the plastic hibiscus from her head and handed it to me with both hands as if it were an injured bird. I untangled some of the fine hairs from the metal clip and pocketed them. I had a box back in our tiny apartment with hairs like these. Perhaps I could reconstruct her someday. Isabel reached out to the cave wall and flattened her palms against its granite. Cave water mapped across the back of her hands to her forearms, where it changed direction and dripped off the bony tips of her elbows onto the hard-packed dirt floor.

"The amazing thing is there's no faucet," she said. "Cave water just happens. It's the cleanest water there is."

"I think glacier water might be cleaner," I said.

"But this water is two hundred years old. It filters through all the rock." She kicked the muddying ground. "If it's all the same to you, I feel different-different, like maybe something inside me is facing the right direction." She took back her flower and searched her scalp for the next best spot to clip. "Soon I'll need double-sided tape." She laughed.

I showed her the hairs I had buried away in my pocket. "Put these back?" I asked.

"You know, after treatment, my hair probably won't grow back the same. Straight hair grows back curly."

"I've never heard that before."

"And it can even change color," she said. "Imagine that."

I ran my hands through my own hair like it was a stranger's. "That's weird."

She flipped make-believe locks around her tilted head. "No, it's exciting—can you picture me with red hair? I'd look more like my sister."

"You would, but I don't want that," I said.

I held out Isabel's hairs, closer this time. "Throw these out then?" Isabel took the straightest, blackest hair from the collection and wrapped it just above the second knuckle on my index finger. Its tensile strength surprised me as my fingertip gorged with blood and began its slow turn to purple. I showed the other cave dwellers all the hope in my bourgeoning finger. "You're welcome," I told the room. Only about half the cave dwellers bothered to even look up.

Isabel twirled in the open space between the tables that lined the cave wall. "Can you imagine such a thing?" She twirled as a perpetually dizzy person twirls, all cockeyed and pinball, ding-dinging between the cave wall and me. She clipped a card table holding a game of checkers. The checkers vibrated like superheated atoms on the board. Two old men in white cowboy hats playing cribbage across the room stopped to watch. They took sips of cave water from Tijuana glassware that they refilled from the dripping ceiling. I couldn't tell if they were empathetic to Isabel or bothered by her heaves and dance and heaves and dance. The caves echoed everything. I stared at the two men until they turned their expressionless faces back to their cards.

"I used to come here when I was a girl," Isabel said. "We could have gone to the ocean, I suppose, but we thought we belonged here. We'd spend Saturday mornings at Grant Rea Park, and by noon, when the monkey bars started to burn our legs, we came here to swim."

Railroad ties eyebolted together shored up the length of the cave that ran thirty-five feet. Portable heaters helped to regulate a temperature thirty-five feet underground that never climbed above sixty degress. The walls seeped water continuously, or they wept, depending on whom you asked. Almost every inch of wooden beam and cribbing was filled with scratch graffiti: Vangi heart Arnie. Becky heart Chewie. Rest in Peace Loca, you could spiral a football, and that nasty Left Arm of God, Sandy Koufax, could throw a 12–6 curveball inside—there was that much space. The cave narrowed down to a four-foot ceiling at the far end, an area fenced off by chicken wire–wrapped rebar cemented into Yuban coffee cans. And just beyond the homemade *No Trespassing* sign was the black hole. This was where the graffiti hearts stopped.

Everyone had his or her place in the cave. The old Mexican men stood on plywood sheeting, bent as withered juniper in the corners of the cave, some with arched backs and propped up on canes made from unused lumber or a felled branch, some still bearing the buds of unborn fruit. They breathed in deeply, using cupped palms to scoop the surrounding cave air into their gaped mouths. They had first dibs on everything. There was an understanding in the cave that gave way to all the mothers and abuelitas, and most everyone gave up their chairs accordingly. The oldest Mexican men were too proud to take a handout. They leaned uncomfortably against the wall until they had to shift to rest their bony hips or their sharpened shoulder blades. They came for their Parkinson's and the nerve-pain gift that was the shitstorm handed down by multiple sclerosis. They came to treat the gout and the stenosis spines that curved similarly to the dried-up narrows. They came to the caves so the deadly radon gas could take away the arthritis that had crippled and bridged their joints into knots. A blind man from Boyle Heights splashed the cave water into his eyes during his stay. He'd talk the whole time about how he couldn't wait to see us all for the first time, that we'd be the most beautiful people in the world.

Some just wanted to be surrounded by the plumerias and birds-of-paradise planted around four cabin-like structures Mr. Gannon had built to accommodate those coming from out of town. From there, the cave dwellers could wave to all their dead friends and relatives buried in Rose Hills. The higher your family plots were located on the hill, the more pull you had at the caves. At least that was the game.

Isabel came for her cancer, or rather, to offset the symptoms of her treatment. Her doctor had drawn her disease process on an oversized clipboard holding graph paper, like he was her coach. He X'd and he O'd the development of her body's decision to attack itself in a way that resembled an offensive alignment in the red zone. Isabel had been reduced to a small blue dot on the board behind a wall of large circles that represented her immune system. One by one the doctor licked his finger and erased a circle. His tongue blued each time until he finally smeared Isabel away under his large thumb pad. He had even gone so far as to call her chance for survival a *trick play*, and that even though victory was not likely, Isabel could gain some level of respect with a real push during the *last drive*. Dr. Gutiérrez had obviously never been a coach. Had he been, he would've known that there are no good losses, no goddamn moral victories. It is hard to say if the gas really helped Isabel. It was tangible on a periodic table, so it was good enough for her to give it a whirl.

Saturday was pets day. It was the day you realized just how many three-legged dogs and cats there really were in Los Angeles. Some had no front or rear legs at all, just crude wheels strapped to their bodies like canine hot rods. Every once in a while there was a border collie with sweet rims that rolled around like she owned the place. Peed on everything like she had blown a gasket. They missed eyeballs and had chewed-away ears from alley fights. Pet owners brought their animals here because they felt guilty, hoping stupidly that the radon might actually make their limbs grow back. They brought the sickest pets swaddled in blankets and tucked in red wagons. These were the pets with large tumors growing off their necks, or completely fogged-out eyes, with no memory of running down the mailman. The caves, in this instance, were for the families. Dying pets in Montebello usually met with a twenty-two behind the ear, or a tricky brick to the head while eating a discarded bean burrito. These families hoped for the slightest chance at a turnaround. (If I come back to this world as a dog, and I get the carnitas platter from Rafael's instead of the normal two cups of Purina, I'm sure as hell gonna look over my shoulder the whole time I eat.)

The Saint Jude Hands of Healing Caves did not allow children inside, so they stood just beyond the cave entrance, behind a spray-painted red line, and watched their pets sleep in the dark, cool corners for the afternoon, or beg for pity scraps from the cave dwellers, something more to eat than the orange peels that littered the dirt floor. The more aggressive dogs tug-of-warred with lizards, pulling them apart to the children's hollers. Lizard parts grew back, but no one really gave a shit about them.

There was no healing gas in my childhood, but the neighborhood did come to my house for miracles. Every street had their miracle slinger, or curandera. On my block, this was my nana. She'd wake up in the morning and make my tata and me homemade tortillas and fried eggs over red chile with pork. After we were squared away, she began to heal the block. Sometimes it meant collecting clothes for the skid row homeless downtown, or crocheting winter hats for abandoned AIDS babies that stacked up in the backyard like cordwood. She burned through rosaries like racing tires.

"Nana had a collection of small bones that she said belonged to Saint Teresa," I said. "Toe bones. A second-class Vatican relic she used to heal the block."

"Did they look like toe bones?" Isabel asked.

"I suppose. They were small enough to be toe bones," I said. I pointed to my own toe. "Small enough that I swallowed one for no good reason."

"You swallowed a bone?"

"Saint Bone," I said.

"Why did you do that?"

"I was that age."

The mothers in the neighborhood brought their children to meet me that summer. Playing kickball or smear the queer with me somehow acted as a blessing. Some of the kids shook my hand, but they never looked me directly in the eye. To them I was the fragile kid with the holy bone floating around inside him. In reality, no one could really tell that I had two hundred and seven bones instead of the standard-issue two hundred and six. But kids sense these differences and respond as kids do.

"Did it work?" asked Isabel. "Did it actually heal anything?"

"I'm pretty sure it fixed Joe."

Isabel motioned me out of the way for the plastic trash can under the card table. She threw up green bile. The hibiscus clip attached to Isabel's hairs flipped over each time she wretched into the can and smacked the top of her head. She used my handkerchief to wipe mucus off the edge of the table. The men with white cowboy hats ignored her this time. "Do you still think I'm pretty?"

Fist into the air.

My uncle Joe had been diagnosed with a brain tumor. Nana made me go with Joe wherever he went that entire summer—the grocery store, to work at the docks all the way in San Pedro on light duty. Not as a companion, but more as a mobile healing relic, a modern-day novena-will-travel. I saw more Dodgers games that summer then I ever had. Joe even took me on his dates. Carmen Yanez worked the ice cream counter at Newberry's and had the key to *Ms. Pac-Man* and *Space Invaders*. I'd play in the arcade for free, a holy toe bone deep inside my body, blessing my high score, while my uncle tasted his favorite flavor of the day. "Carmen Yanez was the very first naked woman I ever saw."

"Touching," said Isabel.

I hated using words like *first*. I know it made Isabel think of *last*.

"I think so. She was always nice to me." And even after Joe broke up with her, she always let me play a game or two if I didn't have enough quarters.

For me, it was the summer of hiding in car trunks and pitch-black closets during dates. I can still smell the exhaust and hear the moans of girls he told me to call Aunt Lola when standing in line at 7-Eleven—*You want Hot Wheels, mijo, you gotta do your part, or you get Matchbox, and Matchbox ain't no kinda ride.* And then in late September, he went to the doctor. The tumor was gone. No trace at all. His oncologist blamed it all on a film snafu. That was the last year the Dodgers won the World Series, 1988. I know because we went to all the home games as my reward for saving him. It was the least he could do, right? He arranged for me to run the bases after the last home game, and when it was time to leave, we just sat in the car until we were the last two people left in the parking lot. Joe didn't say a word through the entire postgame. He sobbed as the last set of sweeping headlights left Solano Canyon into downtown.

"So he dragged you around for a summer while he got treatment."

"Don't you see?" I asked. "He was on a mission to live. He put the science aside and put his faith into something else." I reached down and picked up a handful of the riverbed sand. I held it out to Isabel and let it all slip out from between my fingers.

"Obviously, they mixed up the film," said Isabel. "It happens."

"It doesn't."

"Tell me then," she said. "What do you think's going on here, these caves and healing gas? Because I don't see any toe bones." She poked my stomach. "Unless somewhere in there you're still hiding one." It embarrassed me that my gut felt rich—fat, really—to the sick look of her sucking midsection. "C'mon," she insisted, "you've never mixed up film?"

"That's a sin," I said.

I became a radiology technician because it was the human equivalent of Superman—lead is my weakness. To look inside something, straight through its core, has always appealed to me. I became obsessed with the X-ray after my summer with Joe, the idea of being able to see the bones in my body, including that floating holy metatarsal. It made me believe in something I couldn't see with my own eyes. So I bought old X-rays at garage sales when I could find them and hung them in my bedroom window: a baby's deformed soft-boned wrist, a thirty-five-year-old man's greenstick tibia, and an eighty-something's broken hip illuminated my room. I'd change out body parts over time to fill out the gaps in age. Instead of a sunrise to greet me every morning, I insisted on a self-portrait of my own decay backlit by Jor-El's yellow sun. This made me good at my job, empathy-riddled, and a decent man to my patients. During training, my team leader, an elder statesman, so to speak, in the radiology world, told me that it was my bedside manner that would allow me to do the job for many years to come, that it was how I touched my patient with a gloveless hand that showed them I was their equal, that I was as susceptible as they were, and how I could be more than a cog in the healing process, but the actual healing itself. Like language stuffed into a baby's mouth, I understood this intuitively.

The lead apron was fifteen pounds of dead weight that signaled to the patient something imminent and invisibly toxic was about to pass through their body. Patients didn't want to look vulnerable, so I did my best to play down its necessity, saying that though it did stop stray particles, it was mostly a liability issue protecting the both of us. By the time I had said this, the weight of the shield had already taken their breath away, and it was far too late to explain the delicacy of the X-ray. So, from behind a partition, I looked through a window that was no bigger than a cracker box. This was the moment that a barely audible clicking sound separated what they had known before the X-ray and what they knew after. When Isabel says that film gets mixed up, I disagree. It is the one thing I take great pride in controlling. What does get mixed up is the indecipherable *us*, and how empathy can lull you into fucking your girlfriend's sister, Yolanda, the unbroken version of the woman you loved, while attending her second cousin's quinceañera at the Red Onion in Riverside. That is a mix-up of meteoric proportions. Isabel knew I was attracted to her sister in the same way I was attracted to her way back when. There's no good to come out of the world knowing any of this, so it stayed with me, floating around with no real home. Now every time I located broken things with blasts of concentrated high energy, I felt I had knowledge that wasn't easily digestible in my relationship, like finding a tumor when you're only looking to identify a minor stress fracture.

Sure, I am a lot of things.

The cave's speaker system hissed for a minute before "Chariots of Fire" began to play at top volume. This was the song that played when the second three-hour session had ended, signaling to us in the cave that the park was closing for the day. The human body can only take so much radon and use it for healing purposes before it starts to turn sinister. Each cave dweller was allowed no more than thirty hours of radon per year. Three hours per visit was the permissible business model time frame. This was one hundred and seventy-five times greater than the national standard exposure numbers, but those were numbers that owner Don Gannon simply called jealous math. Mr. Gannon wasn't your stereotypical rancher, stomach lapping over his belt, jeans suspendered up. There was no ten-gallon anything. Mr. Gannon was a thin man in his seventies, who always wore a long-sleeved shirt and shiny polyester vest, no matter the temperature. He had a deep tan that he said was his Chippewa blood rushing to the surface for a fair fight. The creases in his jeans were clean and spoke to the business side of shit-kicking. If it weren't for the two missing fingers on his right hand, I would guess he never spent much time wrangling anything.

He greeted every cave dweller. He helped the abuelitas to their feet and knew them by name: *Ah, the hair on you, Señora Nuanes. Ah, the most beautiful ojos, Señora Boullosa.* He loved the food they brought him during the day, the roasted green Hatch chile and pork, the mole and tamales, the menudo that he said took some getting used to, but he could imagine a day when he wouldn't be able to go without it. He always gave them back their empty dishes washed. During holidays, he'd buy them brand-new sets of Tupperware. The women would trade the different colored containers among themselves. The men gripped his three fingers and shook his hand like the old friends they had become, always patting his back as they walked past. Mr. Gannon smiled at Isabel and reached out to escort her from the cave.

"Isabel, right?"

"Yes, Mr. Gannon," she said.

"Don will be fine."

I jumped Isabel's conversation. "How do you explain the river emptying out the way it did?"

Mr. Gannon sized me up. He excused himself to help the last of the cave-dweller viejas negotiate the muddy exit. He guided them to the single-track path that led to the parking lot. Isabel gave me her look, similar to the look I got the morning after the quinceañera. The sun was dropping down behind the Montebello foothills. The oil pumps on the horizon were mechanical horses with rusted joints that dipped their heads to drink from a mile down, then barely up again. Isabel and I watched them until the sun filled the space between their legs and sank away.

"Maybe he can tell us what's happening here," I said. "That's all."

"Let's just get our things and go." Isabel rolled up her towel.

Mr. Gannon stood at the cave entrance with a clipboard, making small checks on a two-page list. He had to account for each client to be sure no one hid under a tablecloth or behind a bookshelf to steal that bonus fourth hour of radon. I told Isabel to take a seat on a nearby bench, to give me a minute and then we'd leave. I helped Mr. Gannon straighten chairs and put away the *Battleship* games— the Bermuda Triangle had taken out the Pacific Fleet. *Monopoly* had Lego blocks instead of silver treasure pieces.

"There're thieves among us," I said. I held out my hand. "My name is Martin. I'm with Isabel."

"You can't expect to have a cave full of desperate people and not be missing game pieces. Things come and go from the cave," Mr. Gannon said. "It's a funny thing around here. When people feel better, the game pieces come back. Missing books find their way to the empty shelves. Or they don't. There's always something else to use. You ever go to the beach and pick up a seashell, or on a hike and pocket a shiny rock? It's the same thing, Martin. They're reminders of place." He pointed to the six empty tables like he was addressing a room full of ghosts. "You won't find more resourceful people than this group."

I wet my towel against the cave wall and wiped down the tables.

"You were saying something about the water here?"

"Where did it all go?" I asked.

Mr. Gannon grabbed a rake and ran its teeth across the dirt floor, pulling out the debris of the day—some trash, but not enough trash that you might say the cave dwellers were trashy people. Orange peels. The pattern on the floor reminded me of the Zen garden kit I had bought Isabel after she was diagnosed. I had told her it would calm her anxiety about being sick, that all she had to do was make patterns in the sand that resembled ocean water and wind. I bought it the week after I had slept with Yolanda, thinking it might help me focus, to get me back on track. But it was as though she sensed my deviation in our course, away from the *us* that had been taking a beating day after day with no end in sight. Instead, Isabel took up smoking for the sole purpose of using her Zen garden as an ashtray. Cigarette butts raised up like mighty Zen-smoked bamboo from the sand instead. The tiny tools and smooth rocks included in the kit were nowhere to be found. It was her commentary on the state of things. I never said anything to her. I assumed it was how Zen worked, and I swore that, in the background of it all, I could hear the sound of one hand clapping.

"Everyone knows we are at the end of an ice age," Mr. Gannon said. "If you look on a radon potential map, we are in what's called a Mesozoic basin—that is to say two hundred million years of dinosaur fossils were packed into the sedimentary rock around these parts."

"Ha, dinosaurs!" said Isabel.

"All over these parts. And, over an eon, their rotting bodies gave way to the breakdown of the uranium that off-gasses radon. At some point, that ice age clock has to wind itself back up and start its slow freeze all over again."

"I suppose you only get one shot in a lifetime," I said. "That doesn't explain how an entire river valley turned up dry overnight."

"I suppose lava tubes are to blame," Mr. Gannon said. "All that supercooling and superheating. Lava flows and then cools into rock when it hits water. It forms tubes where the lava still flows inside until they empty out and leave a whole maze of tunnels. It's likely one cracked open during a quake. Or just broke apart. The water just found the easy path out."

"Seems you've bottled a miracle, Mr. Gannon. Our Lady of Guadalupe stuffed into your bank account."

"Not gonna lie. The ice ages have made me a rich man." He smiled. "But that's the course of all things."

"That's enough, Martin," Isabel said. "Tell him, Mr. Gannon. That radon gas healing is scientific."

"True, it's scientific. Human science, that is."

Isabel smiled her smile. "See?"

"Then why do you call it Saint Jude's Hands of Healing Caves?"

"So you Mexicans will come," Mr. Gannon said. "Respectfully. You tell me who else would believe in something you couldn't smell, see, hear, or touch. It goes against everything we know as humans. But you do. This community does. And I admire that. I'll tell you this much, it's a damned good business, and likely as close to a miracle as you're gonna get. There are realities that human knowledge cannot wrap its head around, and that leaves faith to explain. That is the one thing my clients bring, the one thing I can't provide."

"I've only ever seen it the other way around," I said. "The miracles."

"Human science," said Isabel.

I shrugged her off.

"I'm careful to include in the brochure that this here gas is pure poison, so to speak. It will take its toll if you swallow a whole mess." He looked to Isabel. "The tricky thing is, it works." He helped Isabel to her feet. "I've been in the radon business since before both of you were born. I've seen all kinds of pain disappear, hands like mummified claws open again. Useful hands." Mr. Gannon pocketed his three fingers into the open slot in his vest. "That's all anybody wants—usefulness. Dogs want to run in an open field. It brings people together. There's no stopping that." Mr. Gannon looked out over the dry and heavily rooted riverbed, the lighted skyline of Pico Rivera to the southwest, the rush of the 60 over his shoulder. "I'd be lying to you if I told you I thought this business would ever bring me to Los Angeles."

Mr. Gannon picked up a rock and threw it into the overgrowth alongside the bank. "Reminds me of my childhood."

Isabel and I both must have looked confused because Mr. Gannon started to laugh.

"Tarzan," he said, pointing toward El Monte. "Tarzan lives down that way."

Isabel grabbed my hand as though we were dealing with a straight-up crazy man who might have fooled the world. "I'm not sure what you mean, Don," she said.

"The first Tarzan movie was filmed a few miles from here, upriver where there used to be a lion sanctuary. They had a show in the old days where a pretty girl like you would stick her head in the lion's mouth. I bet Tarzan would swing right in here and make you his Jane." Isabel would turn the world on its head to be Tarzan's Jane. Even in the faded light, I saw the strawberry blush hit her cheeks.

Mr. Gannon took out his flashlight and pointed its beam into the trees. "They filmed all the Tarzan movies right here in the 1920s. This area was Africa's doppelgänger back in the day. The origin of man right here in the San Gabriel riverbed. So, when this land came up for sale, with radon stamped on it like a personal invitation, there really was no choice but for me to buy every square inch."

"I had no idea," I said. "This has always just been Marrano Beach."

"Pig Beach," Isabel added.

"A shitty watering hole that our grandparents were forced to come to way back when." I turned to Isabel, who seemed genuinely fascinated. "Who knew this was our birthplace."

Lights from a vehicle above us in the parking lot cut across the tops of the trees. We heard two men cursing, then the sound of metal slamming down on metal.

"What was that?" I expected to hear the breaking of glass and quickly took inventory in my head as to what I had inside my car. The voices quieted. The vehicle drove away.

"I was afraid that might happen," Mr. Gannon said.

"What?" I asked. "That what might happen?"

"City vehicle. They locked the parking lot gate."

Isabel started to shiver. We hadn't packed for an evening out. I pulled a red-and-white checkered tablecloth off a card table and draped it over her shoulders. I ran up to the parking lot. Mr. Gannon was already at the gate, giving the padlocked chain a good tug. Finally he gave up and shook his head at the eight-foot chain link fence. "You are welcome to stay here for the night," he said. "The cabins aren't finished, but they got what you'll need for the night. The mattresses were delivered yesterday, so there's that. Still covered in plastic."

"I think we should probably call someone," I said. "I'm sure there's a number."

"City hours," said Mr. Gannon.

"I want to stay," Isabel said. "Why not?"

I could easily think of a thousand reasons why not to stay. It seemed I was always shining a light on Isabel's sickness, giving it too much room for its song and dance on what was supposed to be our stage.

"It's so quiet, like we're in the middle of nowhere," she added.

She said we should try.

Mr. Gannon brought out a laundry basket full of clothing. "Lost and found," he said. "There're a few coats here to choose from." He tapped the toe of his boot near Isabel's sandaled foot. "Pair of tennis shoes at the bottom. Put them on." He looked me over. "Get yourself something."

"I'm fine," I said, while dressing Isabel. "You get as many layers on as you can," I told her.

Mr. Gannon closed the cave for the night. He closed the custom-made welded rebar gate that fit the exact dimensions of the cave's mouth. He turned off the industrial lamps strung up along the cave wall. They clicked off hard like they had an opinion on all things from the day. The blackness of the riverbed overcame us all, and we were reduced to voices until our eyes drew in the faint shine of the moon and city lights.

"Let me get you two in for the night," said Mr. Gannon.

The cabin was nothing more than an unfinished garden shed. The kind you might store a lawn mower or table saw inside. The roof had a slight pitch to keep the rain from pooling. Only the door had a window, and much like inside the cave, the floor was dirt. Mr. Gannon wheeled a small backup generator to the entrance. He checked the gas with his finger, then topped it off. It wasn't uncommon for city electricity to go out for no reason. If you lived in Montebello, you knew that streetlights and signals picked the least opportune time to take a smoke break, usually during rush hour or on a long walk home down Washington Boulevard at two in the morning. He flipped the light switch on and off several times before he was satisfied. The mattress lay in the middle of the shed, propped up on two sawhorses.

"I was hoping to get the floors finished by now."

"This will work fine," I said. Isabel and I lowered the mattress to the ground and peeled away the plastic on one side. "I hope that's okay."

"The maiden voyage," Mr. Gannon said. He handed me the key and winked like he had just checked us into the Saint Jude's Hands of Healing Caves honeymoon suite. "If you need anything, I'm in the beat-up Airstream at the top of the trail."

"You're a kind man," Isabel said.

"Okay then. Make yourselves right at home." The beam from Mr. Gannon's flashlight bounced along the trail as he made his way back up to the parking lot. Isabel and I stood in the starlight and stared at one another. I tried to take her hand, but it seemed as though the excitement of the day was falling behind us. She was tired again and reminded that we weren't in this place for a vacation, that no matter the distractions of the day, the fact was she was broken in places that would take an eternity to heal—or yes, a miracle. But the simple fact was that she has always been whole, and I have been the puzzle broken into a thousand pieces. And I am not sure if some of those pieces just might have been lost under the couch somewhere. I was the last person to have seen the complete version of me. I needed to start putting me all back together again, starting with the outside edge.

The cabin had the smell of a bunch of power tools left in a room for a long time. That is to say it smelled electrical. Isabel shuffled across the room and kicked up a plume of sawdust. She sat on the edge of the mattress, staring at the bare studded wall like it was a Picasso. It was warm enough inside that I considered taking off the extra clothing. Isabel pulled her lost-and-found pea coat up around her chin and buttoned the neck collar.

"Here," I said, holding out my jacket. "You can have mine if you're too cold."

"I don't want to stay in here," said Isabel.

"We could've called someone by now, but you—"

The plastic under the mattress crackled as Isabel leaned across to put her finger on my lips. "I want you to take me back inside the cave."

Look at her look at me. I am the one.

Mr. Gannon had one small light on at the far back of the trailer, in the space I imagined he slept. He couldn't see down into the wash to the cave entrance from where the trailer sat at the edge of the parking lot. But it wasn't Mr. Gannon's line of sight that worried me. It was his intuition that held me in place at the top of the riverbank, looking for any movement. I only blinked when Isabel pulled on my shirt and flashed a light in my eyes.

"Look what I found in the toolbox," she said, handing me a penlight.

"Be careful with that." I pulled her hands down to her side. "Keep it in your pocket." I looked back to the trailer that was now dark.

The rebar gate to the caves didn't take too much undoing before it opened. It dragged along the sandy riverbed, leaving a small trench behind its swing. The cave was darker than I had expected. And standing in place a few moments made no difference. We couldn't see much farther than a few feet beyond our reach. "Are you there?" Isabel searched the open black space around her.

"Your light," I said. Isabel tested her light on and off before handing it to me. It read *Manuel's Automotive* on its side. I bet Manuel would get a kick out of us using his light right now to sneak into a cave full of radon gas under the cover of night. "Remind me to call Manuel."

"Who?" Isabel asked.

"Your guardian angel." I showed Isabel the side of the light. Without the cave dwellers, Saint Jude's Hands of Healing Caves was just another hole in the ground, and graffitied much like the pillars under the San Gabriel Bridge. It was wet everywhere—under our feet, above our head, and the walls seeped out more cave water than I had remembered. The air even felt wet, and when I breathed in, my lungs expanded heavily and pulled down in my chest like water balloons hanging from a spout.

"Can you feel the air?" I asked Isabel.

She took in tiny gulps. It looked like she was trying to separate the water from the radon from the air. "That's healing," she said.

"Why are you breathing like that?"

She cupped her hands under her armpits. She pressed against her sides as she inhaled. "I love feeling the heavy air inside me."

"It's so humid in here."

We walked down a makeshift ramp toward the back of the cave, where Mr. Gannon stored extra wheelchairs donated to him by Beverly Hospital. Most of the chairs had a squirrely wheel or ripped seat padding, but nothing that kept Mr. Gannon from knowing a good deal when he saw it. They were well cleaned. And probably run through a ten-point inspection. A cable ran through the spokes of the wheelchairs and locked into an eyebolt drilled into the cave wall. Isabel sat down in the last chair next to the chicken wire fencing.

"Is this what you wanted, to get another dose for the day?"

"I love us in here, is all." Isabel knocked on the wall. "All this rock. It feels safe."

I wanted to argue radon gas and show her the spreadsheet in the brochure that clearly stated we were now in the red section, the part with the cartoon skull and crossbones, but the sound of the cave wall cracking open behind Isabel stopped me. I pulled her from the wheelchair as a section of rock calved off and came down right where she had been sitting, taking her place in the chair. With the penlight, it was hard to tell if the wheelchair was completely crushed or just pushed into the muddy ground. The sound inside the cave was deafening. With only one exit, it echoed off every angle of the cave wall before finally releasing to the outside. We were covered in mud. I made a quick assessment of Isabel, bending all her parts. I knew every curve of every bone known to man. I knew exactly how each bent, how each broke, and the amount of time it took for each to heal, so it didn't take me long to know that she was physically okay. "You all right?"

Isabel wiped mud from her face and nodded as the overhead lights clacked on. The last three bulbs on the strand above our head were burned out. Mr. Gannon knocked over two tables to get to the back of the cave. He looked at the amount of water now pooling on the cave floor in large circles. He lifted his boots and watched his footprints fill with water and disappear into larger connecting puddles. He grabbed towels from a plastic bin next to where the cowboys had spent their day. I could still see them shaking their heads. I puffed out my chest.

"Dry off," said Mr. Gannon. "What are you doing in here?"

"I wanted to come back," said Isabel. "It's my fault."

Mr. Gannon looked down at the wheelchair. He got down on his knee to inspect the damage up close. He broke off a piece of rock sitting in the chair and rubbed it between his good fingers like he was reading braille. "Could've killed you, Isabel."

Isabel looked overhead before stepping closer to the fencing.

"That's far enough," said Mr. Gannon. "It's not safe in here, c'mon."

"Listen," said Isabel. "That sounds like water."

I pointed to the ground and to the water dripping off the ceiling.

"No," she said. "In the black hole. It sounds like a river flowing." Isabel leaned into the chicken wire that now looked like cheap twine netting struggling with her weight. The cemented Yuban cans lifted on one side. I grabbed her waistband and twisted her sweat pants in my fist to cinch her close to me. She reached out her hand. "Give me the penlight."

"This is ridiculous, Isabel. Let's go, *now*."

She turned to me and held her hand out higher. "I know you won't let go," she said. "I just want to see something."

I handed her the light. She bent the chicken wire fence down from the top without much effort. I grabbed hold of her with two hands as she stretched out over the hole. She shined the light down as far as she could reach. I could hear the faint sound of turbulent water. "Can you see anything?" I asked.

"Nothing," she said. "Hold tight."

Isabel turned the penlight around. It lit up her face. And between the streaks of mud, I could still see a hint of blush in her cheeks. "Yes," I said. "I still think you're pretty." I wasn't even sure Isabel heard me, but Mr. Gannon took hold of my waistband like all this might actually be worth a damn. Isabel hovered out over the fence. She held the penlight out between two fingers. Her lips moved, but there was no sound. I assumed she made a wish because then she dropped her guardian angel straight down into the black hole and watched it fall away, child-eyed.

"Could you see anything down there?" asked Mr. Gannon.

"Just the light. It fell straight down and then disappeared."

"Lava tubes," Mr. Gannon said. "Sounds like the only explanation."

"Maybe fifty feet or so," said Isabel.

I pulled Isabel up and gave her my towel to cover her head. I had to muscle my own release from Mr. Gannon's grip. He stepped around Isabel to get a look into the black hole. "The water table is slowly rising under here, and it's beginning to cut away at all this dirt and rock. All this seeping."

"What does it mean?" I asked.

"It means this place is gonna be full again," he said. "And real soon."

It was difficult to see anything now at the back of the cave. Isabel crouched down, obviously fascinated by the possibility of the water returning.

"What's that smell?"

Mr. Gannon pulled down the strand of lights from the middle of the cave and held the bulbs over his head to see where the wall had broken away. "That's the smell of the ice age," he said. "Take a look."

What looked like the base of a log jutted out a foot from the cave wall. Isabel shook her head. "Is that moss?"

"That's a ten-thousand-year-old hairdo," said Mr. Gannon. "It had to be a hard, cold pack to be preserved this well."

"Old slaughterhouse bones?" I asked.

"A mammoth tusk."

"How did that get here?" asked Isabel.

"It walked here," said Mr. Gannon. He laughed and pulled Isabel in for a closer look. "To find something like this so far south is nothing to sneeze at."

"Kids found pig bones down here all the time," I said. I prompted Isabel to agree with me from her days spent swimming here. I wasn't even sure if that was true or not, but it was my only response to such a find, to explain it away with something useful to me.

"I've never found anything down here until now," she said.

"I'm a rancher before anything else. I know pig bones. And unless pigs in the 1920s were ten feet tall, I'd say this here's a prehistoric find."

In the dimmed cave light, the tusk had a smattering of sepia. It was charred black at its opening, and packed with a red clay. It disappeared into the cave wall and reappeared eight feet away, its once sharp end now dulled and pointing out and upward three feet to the cave ceiling. Threadlike cracks gave the tusk a scrimshaw appearance, a snapshot of a million yesterdays. The space between the two points seemed like impossible earth to cut through. Mr. Gannon kicked the wall with his black boot, leaving a streak of polish on the granite.

"A cave drawing," I said.

"She's in there pretty deep," he said. "That curve could go as far as two or three feet.

"Tell me where to dig," said Isabel.

Mr. Gannon walked Isabel to a plastic lawn chair. "I think you should sit this one out. No telling what will happen."

Mr. Gannon handed me a rock that looked especially shaped for carving away the earth around the tusk. It was the perfect primal tool for the task. I stabbed at hard-packed dirt. I pictured early man in the first Home Depot, staring down the long aisles filled with a variety of sharpened rocks. It took over an hour to expose a two-foot section. None of us could say as to how long we had been in the caves. The smell was overwhelming, a rotten-meat mold. Ancient flesh. I had never smelled anything like it. Isabel breathed in deeply. I expected her to throw up again, but she didn't. Instead she pushed away from the chair and began to dig with me, her hand over of mine as we pressed and cut our way through.

I wanted to share this moment with all the cave dwellers. I wanted to give back the gift of work to their useful and pain-free hands. One hundred abuelitas with molcajete stones, grinding away at the cave wall in prayer, telling their stories as though they were preparing a great meal for the dead. I wanted them to know that their river was coming back to them. That it was bringing everything since the beginning of time with it.

Most of the dirt had been cleared when Mr. Gannon anchored in his foot the best he could in the mud. He slipped the narrow end of the mammoth tusk between the empty spaces in his hand and pulled against the ten-thousand-year-old decay, roots that resembled an old woman's crooked bent-bow knuckles. I squatted underneath the tusk and reached up to hold it in place. The cave-wall water ran the length of my arm and down my sleeves into my pants. It didn't seem like it would ever give way until its own weight began to rip it out from the wall. The large end hit the ground first. I lowered down its dull tip. The three of us stood over the tusk, not sure how to welcome it into this world. Isabel cleared the clay from inside. "I can fit my entire arm in." We raised the mammoth tusk up on its end. Even with such an exaggerated curve, it was taller than us by two feet and scratched the cave roof. Isabel positioned it between her legs and teased the loosening tufts of rancid hairs. "I can't wait to see how these grow back," she said. She took off her hibiscus clip and attached it to the base. She tipped the tusk toward me. "This is yours," she said, "to replace what you've lost."

I leaned the tusk into my body and squatted it up onto my shoulder to carry it out to the cave entrance. I felt strong.

Isabel pulled the plastic sheeting out from underneath the mattress. She met me outside, and we wrapped the tusk together. It glowed orange in the early morning light that sifted down through the eucalyptus branches. I sat outside on a flat rock ledge and looked out over the riverbed. I imagined the ghosts of saber-toothed cats gathered in the sage and buckwheat and tall grasses, their barrel chests heaving out long, patient breaths like they've witnessed this before.

Isabel was on her stomach just inside the cave entrance, her ear pressed to the dirt floor. She hummed with the rush of water coursing underground. "Lie down next to me," she said. I was eager to tell her the entire of story of us, as if she hadn't been living it right alongside me this whole time, lighted like a magnificent torch. I kissed her head, ran my hands through her hair. "The floor is ice cold," she said. "I bet if we stay here long enough, we'll freeze in place."

FORTRESS OF SOLITUDE

Daniel had only reached the edge of the sidewalk when Superman pulled up in his '57 Chevy and kicked the passenger-side door wide open. Superman drove thirty-five miles per hour the entire way home. He was as safe as they come, Daniel thought. Superman held his bulking left arm out the driver-side window until he hit the dirt road that zigzagged into La Loma. Dust kicked up into the car window before Daniel could roll his side up. Superman ran his strong finger along the cherry-red dash, leaving a clean line behind it. With his seat belt pulled tightly across his lap, Daniel never took his black-and-blue eye off the Man of Steel, not since the moment they left the parking lot at Solano Elementary, and not when they passed the Elysian Park baseball fields, where all the kids ran to the fence to see if it was really true—Daniel Castillo getting a ride home to Chavez Ravine from Superman himself. And as that brand-new-showroom-floor-candy-cane '57 Chevy they rode in passed the fields, Daniel only stretched out his arms to acknowledge the other children, the tips of his fingers barely brushing the windshield in an overture of flight.

"That teacher of yours, Miss Lorraine," said George, "she's something special for a bunch of second graders."

"She seems nice enough," Daniel said.

Superman smiled at Daniel and adjusted the radio. His teeth, so big and white, could easily bite through a metal girder. Superman tapped the dial gingerly so as not to push his entire hand through the radio and into the engine compartment. Daniel stared out the window as they passed his old school, Palo Verde Elementary. The basketball hoops had already been taken down and Dumpstered. The playground had been broken into large asphalt chunks as though Mole Man had recently smashed out from underneath to pull all the hopscotch and foursquare courts underground.

All the sand in the sandboxes sieved out to fill the empty spaces in the underworld below. City workers stood on the school roof in their hard hats. They used long sickle-bladed tools to scrape off the terracotta shingles that shattered on the sidewalk below. Daniel and his friends had broken out the windows to his old classroom at Palo Verde only the week before. They had emptied a bucketful of old baseballs to cutter-perfect circles through the glass panes from sixty feet away. Daniel felt guilty over the whole thing now, with Superman like a stone pillar next to him, sitting behind the wheel in a three-piece suit.

A bulldozer pushed dirt into the abandoned far end of school where the roof had already been removed. "They aren't even gonna tear the school down," Daniel said. "My dad says they'll fill it like a poor man's grave." Superman dipped his head down to see out the driver-side window. He waved to the bulldozer operator who spit on the ground and gave back a distrustful look. The look said, *Beat it, Big Blue. It's too late for you to save anything here.* Daniel took note and growled.

"How does your father know that?" asked George.

"They filled up plenty of houses up here."

Superman sat back into the Chevy's fine white leather bench seat and surveyed the hillside. A small herd of goats tempered the tall overgrowth that had begun to take over the road. This wasn't Benedict Canyon with all its beautiful Hollywood palaces. These were simple, sturdy homes with brightly colored beams that held them in place. Many had arched entries and latticed porches with flowering hibiscus and mums, ivy that pulled the houses down to the ground and held them in place. Homes in the distance sat in rubble piles like children's blocks waiting to be played with again. Some sat on stilts that watched over the hillside. One had a red door. Skill and practicality transitioned across the roofline horizon, from clean woodwork to corrugated and rusted-out sheet metal. These were working-class family homes.

Makeshift shrines to Our Lady of Guadalupe took up all the space on the sidewalks. There were signs on every corner that begged for fair market deals for land, signs that asked for prayers and that *Walter O'Malley and Dodgers, just leave us alone!*, and signs for all the glorious veteranos. One woman sat outside her home under a pomegranate tree. A picture of two young men leaning on baseball bats, their arms around one another in an embrace, sat pinned down under her bosom. It didn't take a superman to realize the men were brothers, and the woman's sons. War medals hung on particleboard nailed up with two two-by-fours over her head like a lemonade stand. Her sign read: *They Fought for Freedom—Is This the America They Gave Their Lives For?* Superman nodded to the woman as they drove by. She gave a polite wave back. Daniel handed Superman his handkerchief when he noticed the superhero wiping his sweaty palms on his Italian dress pants.

The red Chevy stood out like the scorching sun. It was longer than any car Daniel had ever seen, let alone taken a ride in. If Superman brought the Chevy to top speed, its shark-fin-silver-chrome-tipped rear fenders would keep the car true. A car like this one had been to space and back. Everyone stopped to look as it blazed a trail through town.

"They'll be happy you're here," Daniel said.

"I can't stay too long," said George.

"My father will want to meet you."

"I would hope so," George said. "Can't just have a stranger bring home your son and not shake his hand."

A stranger? How ridiculous, Daniel thought. He hadn't understood most of the day's events: Superman coming to his classroom on the first day of school to sing songs in Spanish during lunch. He spoke better Spanish than any of them. Lorraine had introduced him to the class as Superman, then giggled and called him the actor George Reeves the rest of the day. She explained that he had come to welcome all the new Chavez Ravine students to Solano Elementary. Superman sang and danced and laughed. He carried more books than humanly possible when the new encyclopedia collection he had bought for the library arrived. During kickball, he launched the ball over the cafeteria roof. It had missiled over Daniel's head with a high-pitched whine, and when it finally landed a city block away, Daniel could hear the exploding concrete. It was obvious what was happening, and Daniel had picked up on it right away. What are you supposed to think when a superhero gets dropped into your lap? Daniel didn't speak to Superman the entire day. He wasn't nervous as much as he was curious as to how Superman might go about hiding his identity. And he did it spot on! All the kids called him Mr. Reeves as they lined up for his autograph at the end of the day in Miss Lorraine's classroom. But Daniel knew the Last Son of Krypton when he saw him. When Daniel finally spoke up and asked Superman for the ride home to La Loma, telling him that only he possessed the special powers that could really be put to some good use in Chavez Ravine, Miss Lorraine scolded Daniel and told him not to look a gift horse in the mouth—a phrase completely lost on Daniel not for its meaning but more for its second-grade timing. Daniel was clearly surprised then when Superman pulled to the curb in his red Chevy to give him a ride up, up, and away.

Superman pointed at the graffiti on a water tank as they cruised into La Loma—*¡Vive Carlos Castillo!* "Isn't that your last name?" George asked.

"That's my father, Carlos Mena Castillo." Daniel looked at Superman as if to time his response. "The welterweight champion of La Loma."

"Champion. That's a pretty big title."

"Well, he used to be. It's been a while now."

"I see," George said. "Must have something to do with that shiner you're sporting."

"Kids want to know if I can box."

"Can you?" George asked.

"I never wanted to learn."

Superman shadowboxed inside the Chevy, giving small jabs to Daniel's left side. "I bet you could go twelve rounds in a pinch." Daniel pointed out to Superman his purple and now yellowing eye. He pressed on it until his eyes began to water. Superman put both hands back on the steering wheel. He explained to Daniel how you've got to start somewhere in this life, young man. "I've had my share of lickings, if you can imagine that," said George.

Daniel could not.

Bishop's Road and Effie Street intersected at a single streetlight at the top of a hill where three shirtless boys shot marbles in the hard dirt. A young man smoked and listened to a transistor radio outside his car. Superman waved, and the young man cocked his head back. The road forked to the right and down into La Loma toward Daniel's house. He pointed the way by swaying his outstretched arms in one direction or another, flying shotgun with his eyes closed. Superman made the turns through the neighborhood as though he, too, had flown over Chavez Ravine once or twice before. Daniel sensed this, as one does, one superhero to another. "I know these streets like an old crow," said Daniel. "Stop. Right here."

"That's pretty good," said George. "Couldn't do that if I tried."

Daniel knew that the first rule of Superman was to be humble. The second rule was to do anything he needed to do under the circumstances. The Chevy rolled to a stop at the curb in front of Daniel's house. It had a large porch with a broken cedar fence that surrounded its border. Superman clucked to the chickens under the house. "I had chickens when I was a boy," he said.

"In Kansas?" Daniel asked.

"Little town in Iowa, actually," said George. "Woolstock."

Daniel wasn't sure of the game Superman was trying to play.

A large rooster came out from under the porch to peck at Superman's feet. "You can smash it into the ground if you want," said Daniel. But Superman scooped up the yard bird and gently placed it back under the house. He pushed up a half-cut sheet of plywood to cover the hole. Daniel kicked at the siding, and all the chickens scrambled and flew with their stub wings into the crawl space floor joists. Daniel held a nail to the plywood's edge. He asked Superman to push it in with his thumb as Daniel's father kicked open the screen door.

"Pinche gallos!" Daniel's father yelled. Carlos Castillo had that boxer's strut you see inside the ring just before the first bell. He kept his feet moving even when he told you, *I AM standing still, cabrón*. His head bobbed side to side when he spoke, and his hands had never been properly introduced to the inside of his pants pockets. Cauliflower ears and a calcified chin accounted for most of his face. It was a readiness you can't teach someone who's not interested in hitting a man over and over again under bright lights. Carlos wore his T-shirt with the front pulled over his head, his arms through the sleeves, so he could show off his wiry welterweight chest. Daniel's mother once told him that if his father and the rooster could ever stand shoulder to shoulder, it would be very difficult to tell them apart.

Daniel flipped the nail into the grass. "We're down here."

"We nothing. Get up here, Danny," Carlos said.

Daniel stepped to the front of the house, pulling Superman to his side by his jacket sleeve to explain his day. "I got a ride home from——"

"George Reeves, sir." Superman held his hand out to Carlos. The men shook. "I hope you don't mind, but I gave Daniel a ride home. There was some confusion at the school is all."

Carlos nodded that Mexican nod, a continuous movement that worked to help compute how the world was trying to get over on you. He slapped the back of Daniel's head. "You bothering Mr. George Reeves?"

"Please, Carlos. Mr. Castillo. Daniel wasn't a bother at all." Superman brushed Daniel's hair back. "It was my honor to bring your son home." He pointed to the hillside. "I've never been up here before."

The Chevy taking up most of Spruce Street caught Carlos's eye. "That's a mas chingon ride, George Reeves. Danny, you came home in that car?" Carlos leaned in close to Superman, still shaking his hand, only harder now. "You must get lots of Hollywood starlets in a ride like that." Superman pulled his grip loose. Carlos turned to Daniel. "That's a man's ride, mijo. I met your mother in car like that."

Superman kneeled down and placed his hand on Daniel's shoulder. "I think you may have left your books in the car. Let's get them out for you." Daniel used all his might to pull open the passenger-side door that the carmaker should have considered using only for a barn. He was careful not to scrape the bottom on the curb. Carlos did his boxer dance in the front yard in front of Superman. Daniel could see that his father was nearly two feet shorter than the Man of Steel.

"I think I'll be going," said George.

"Daniel probably told you a lot of things, but he tell you I'm the welterweight boxing champion?" Carlos held up his fists. "They said I had hands made from rock. Eight years, and my back never hit the mat. That's kinda super, huh?" Carlos stepped on the edge of Superman's polished wing tips.

"He told me you used to be," George said. "The champ, that is."

Carlos walked into the middle of the street. Immediately, the hails of *Hey, Champ! Órale, Champ!* came from Genaro's Market a half a block away. "Hear that? Wherever I go in La Loma, my legacy follows." Carlos put his hand on the Chevy's candy-cane front fender and pushed himself up onto the curb. He whispered into Superman's ear. "If you ever want to know what it's like to hit man for reals, you come see me." Carlos grabbed Daniel as he walked between the two men with his books locked in his arms. "Get inside, Danny."

Daniel ran straight through the Mendozas' rose garden and Tito Lopez's junk car lot like his feet were on fire. He ducked through fences and stood on the empty altars in the front yards of abandoned houses to look out over the hillside—all the Saint Judes and Fatimas had packed up and relocated downtown without any say in the matter. He thought that if he just ignored the burning sensation in his chest as he ran, he might catch Superman at the end of Bishop's Road before he jumped onto the highway and was gone forever. Daniel hadn't expected the flashy Chevy to sneak up on him the way it had. And when Superman tipped his hat and pulled his glasses to the tip of his nose, lightning zapped through all the wires in his boy body. Daniel did his best to quiet his heavy breathing. Superman turned off the engine and adjusted the driver's-side mirror to see down the road behind him.

"Take it easy, son," said George. "I think we're in the clear."

"I can't believe I caught you," said Daniel.

"Well, that's because it doesn't happen very often." George laughed. "I stopped for a soda at the little market there by your house. Then I saw you jump from the window and take off running. So, I bought two."

Daniel was well aware of his blistering speed. "How did you find me?"

"You made it easy for me," George said. "I followed the clouds of dust between the houses."

Daniel ducked behind the Chevy and squinted hard into the sun. He rubbed his chest under his shirt, careful not to smudge Superman's polished front bumper.

"He didn't follow me?" asked Daniel.

"No, Daniel. Your father was talking to some official-looking men on the porch when I left."

"They come every week to nail paperwork to the door," said Daniel. "They are forcing us to leave." He exhaled from a deep place in his eight-year-old body. "I don't want to leave here, but sometimes I don't want to stay, either."

Superman bent down to rub the scuff off the tip of his shoe. "I know exactly how you feel," he said.

"What time is it?" Daniel pulled down Superman's arm to look at the gold watch on his wrist. "Come with me."

Superman threw his keys up into the air and snatched them back without even looking. He put them in his pocket and loosened his tie. "Lead the way, young man. But not too fast, I'm an old man."

Daniel tucked his shirt into his jeans and pulled the laces tight on his shoes. For the first time during the day, Daniel noticed the gray hairs on the sides of Superman's head, not that there were a lot, but enough that he wondered how being on this planet had taken its toll on the superhero over the years. Daniel promised he'd take it easy on him. "But you'll have to climb a bit. It's over that hill," Daniel said, pointing in the distance. "We have to hurry before the sun goes down."

Superman rubbed his knee and took off his right shoe to pour out some loose gravel. "I think I've got that much left in me, sport."

They cut through the yards between Reposa Street and Gabriel Avenue until they reached the end of Malvina Avenue. This was where Chavez Ravine opened up to new construction in Elysian Park. Superman ripped his dust-covered suit pants on barbed wire from his left thigh to his ankle. Daniel looked for blood, but not one drop! Superman didn't seem concerned in the slightest.

"We look alike now," Daniel said, pointing to the hole in his own pants leg.

A yellow school bus appeared from around a tight curve at the bottom of the hill where cinder block construction and dump trucks filled the small valley. Superman looked at his watch and showed Daniel the time, tapping the crystal face.

"There's a school down there?" asked George. "It seems awful late for kids to get home."

"We're right on time." Daniel picked up all the rounded stones at his feet. He made a small hammock from the bottom of his T-shirt and began to fill it. "Grab some rocks," he said. "They'll be gone soon." When Daniel's shirt began to tear, he dropped to his haunches. Superman tried to take the same pose, but the pain in his knee was too much. He sat down and crossed his legs Indian style. "I bet you'll recognize most of them."

Superman couldn't sit in one spot for too long. He pushed himself up to his feet and adjusted his glasses. The bus teetered on the dirt road. Men wearing orange jumpsuits bounced in their seats with their heads hung low. There were no windows, only a grated metal screen that made it difficult for Superman to make out their faces.

"They're prisoners," said George. "A busload of prisoners."

"Dead men," said Daniel. "Calaveras. The skulls. . . . Calaveras! Calaveras!" Daniel repeated, over and over as he urged Superman to join in.

"Calaveras!" Superman yelled. A smile formed on his face.

"My grandfather says they aren't even men anymore."

Daniel handed Superman his smoothest and biggest rock. Superman held it at his side the entire time Daniel threw his rocks at the bus. When the prisoners began to yell obscenities at Daniel, they did so as if they knew him well, that they expected Daniel to be on the hillside every day. The *pinche cabróns* and *little fuckers* were mixed with hints of endearment, as if the prisoners saw something of themselves in Daniel throwing his rocks, a moment they have likely come to value after a long day of work, one that took them home when they, too, were young boys. The oldest prisoners never looked up from their feet. Superman told Daniel that they were the men who knew their mistakes better than anyone, redemptive men, and that was a quality not to be taken lightly in a man. He told Daniel that there were more sinners in this world than rocks on the hillside. Daniel agreed, as eight-year-olds do.

Daniel's arm was big-league ready. He arched each stone, accounting for the speed of the bus. He hit the side of the bus like it was a carnival game. The men pounded on their caged windows, promising Daniel the ass beating of the century.

"They come here every day to help build the new police academy," Daniel said. "Sometimes I get them in the morning before school." Daniel tapped his head. "So they think of me all day."

The rock was still in Superman's hand. He rubbed his wedding ring across its rough surface. Daniel waved his hasta mañana fist at the men and sat back down. "Did you see anyone you know?" asked Daniel. "The bank robbers, I bet." Superman nodded. And as the calaveras rounded the last bend before heading down into Lincoln Heights, the superhero finally threw his rock. His fine Italian-made suit jacket made it difficult for him to get a full rotation into his throw. The rock hit the gravel near the back tire and short-hopped up and off the yellow-and-black striped metal siding.

The Man of Steel and Daniel cheered wildly.

They sat on the hill as the sun fell from the sky. From there they could see all the way to downtown, city hall rising up into the early evening stars. The palms and eucalyptus swayed with a breeze that also brought with it the smell of garbage from the nearby dump. All the promises of the Los Angeles cityscape stopped at the freight yards near the highway where the dirt trails fanned out into the hills. Superman pointed to white lights that turned on over the rose-covered shrines. A small procession gathered in front of the Santo Niño church. Women covered their heads with scarves and held up banners. Altar boys balanced wooden boards holding the statues of archangels and tired-looking saints over their heads. A young man sat on a nearby water tower, quietly plucking his guitar. His legs swung with the bending palm fronds. All the damaged and burned-out houses on the outskirts of Chavez Ravine gave way to eight-foot hibiscus and spidering bougainvillea that crept toward the center of town. Daniel held out his hand to match the shadows that fell over Chavez Ravine.

"This is a beautiful place. The flowers alone," George said.

"My father spends more time cutting them down," said Daniel. "He curses at them for taking over everything."

"Do you know what they call a place like this?"

Daniel shrugged.

"Shangri-La," George said. "It's the mystical paradise from a book called *Lost Horizon*. This might just be the most perfect place on earth."

Daniel raised his nose into the air and looked down the hillside toward the dump. "Do they play baseball in Shangri-La?" Daniel asked.

"All year long."

Daniel could see his house from the hillside, just beyond the row of shacks where many of the railyard workers lived. They were only there for short periods of time before moving on to some place else.

"What's your home like, Superman?" asked Daniel.

Superman spun his wedding band around his finger and dug his wing tip heels into the dirt. He pulled at the two frayed ends of fabric to bridge together the giant hole in his pants leg.

"Home," said George.

"The Fortress of Solitude has to be better than this," said Daniel. "That's where I want to be—at the top of the world."

Superman put his glasses into the silk-lined pocket under his lapel. He squinted hard at Daniel. "It's a big place, Daniel. Honestly, it's probably too big for one man."

"I bet men don't nail papers to your door."

"No, no, they don't," George said. "Too much ice at the top of the world for that kind of nonsense."

"That's what I want. A place where none of them will come."

The procession grew down below. Superman pointed to a group of veteranos in their army greens with war medals pinned to their chests, carrying the statues on their war-torn bodies. "Do they ever tell their stories?" he asked.

"Only that the fideo in Korea isn't as good as home," Daniel said. "My tío Gilbert says nothing you'd kill for."

Superman laughed and turned away to wipe his eyes. Daniel could only imagine that the songs and dancing had reached into Superman's heart and softened it some, that as the Last Son of Krypton, he was left with an otherworldly dose of emotion to carry everywhere he went. Simply put, Daniel thought that a star-load of emotion gets squeezed out when you least expect it. He put his hand on Superman's back and told him about how at night he dreamt of the Fortress of Solitude, its long crystal spires jettisoned from the middle of molten Earth, one hundred feet high into the magnetic sky. He drew the image from his dreams in the dirt. Superman gave it a thumbs up and took out his pocketknife to add to the drawing. "Don't forget my bedroom. It opens up to the northern lights." Superman handed Daniel his pocketknife and told him not to lose it, that super-hardened steel is not easy to come by. "Where's that dump?" George asked. He covered his nose when the wind changed direction. "I know it's close." Daniel pointed down the back side of the hill into a section of Elysian Park with no lights or clear trail markings.

"What's at the dump?" asked Daniel.

"The Fortress of Solitude. That's where we're going to build it."

～

Superman lifted the Maytag dryer box over his head and threw it up to Daniel. Maytag boxes were always the heaviest, the thickest cardboard to cut through. Daniel and his friends would come to the dumps to find appliance boxes. They'd cut them open and ride them down the grassy hillside in summer. There weren't many boxes, as most families either rebuilt their existing oven or washing machine, or bought a used one from down the street. Daniel's mother had joked that her refrigerator had been around the world and back, having lived on Yolo Drive, Bouett Street, and way over on Paducah Street. She'd wished she could get out as much, that maybe it would give her a reason to buy a new dress rather than make one. She made clothes for the entire family. She told Daniel he was lucky to grow up in a family just rich enough that she didn't have make his underwear from burlap potato sacks. Daniel had scratched himself at the thought.

"That's a roof-sized box right there, if I've ever seen one," said George.

Daniel sliced down the box seams. The hardened steel cut through the double-walled cardboard like he imagined a heat-vision ray might. The box had an advertisement taped on one side: A blonde woman wearing a fitted yellow sweater and string of pearls around her neck pointed to a banner that read, *Exclusive Halo of Heat—A Gentle and Even-Drying Heat as Safe as Sunshine.* She wore a long white skirt and hovered on her toes in diamond-studded high heels. She looked exactly like Miss Lorraine from Solano Elementary. The two women shared the same red lipstick. Daniel held up the box panel and yelled down to Superman, "Look, it's Miss Lorraine!"

"You can do a lot worse than to share the Fortress of Solitude with that doll," said George.

Daniel agreed and set the panel aside. He couldn't wait to see Miss Lorraine again. He wouldn't tell her, but Daniel knew that he'd picture her in front of the class like she was working the showroom floor at Maytag.

Superman took off his jacket and rolled up the sleeves on his white dress shirt. His thin black tie made for a good headband. Daniel stopped working and waited to see if Superman opened his shirt, to see if he might catch a glimpse of the *S* across his chest. But Superman turned away and headed farther down the hill to where all the old water heaters were lined up and half-buried like missile silos. Only a few homes in Chavez Ravine actually had water heaters, but people from all over Los Angeles often abandoned theirs here. Superman unearthed each cylinder and carried it over his shoulder to the space where Daniel had already removed much of the trash.

"Pillars of ice," George said. "We'll line them up side by side."

Daniel punched his open palm. "Impenetrable!"

"That's a good word," said George.

Daniel took his time to work free a box of Atlas fluorescent bulbs partially hidden under a bag of rotting fruit. He inspected each tube. Superman stripped the bare copper wiring out from an electrical box and tied the bulbs to the ends of four six-foot water pipes. He drove them into the ground at an angle by the entrance. Daniel adjusted the pipes to give them an ice-crystal-recently-speared-out-from-the-core-and-mantle look. The metal pipes were cold to the touch, and Daniel exhaled into his cupped hands every few seconds to keep them warm.

Superman punched out a water heater's two corroded ends to complete the last section of tunnel that ran the length and width of the fortress in a small trench that Daniel had dug out with a bucket for the last hour. He covered the tunnel with the flattened cardboard boxes and flipped old tractor tires on top to anchor it all down. It was impressive enough that he asked Superman to let him know what it looked like from space if he ever got the chance. It seemed impossible that man might ever find his way into deep space to ever do it himself. Space was just a Sunday drive for Superman. Daniel stacked up all the hubcaps he could find on the dirt mound nearest the fortress. Superman bent precisely and hung each hubcap on sheet metal to catch all the light from the southern sky. "You'll reflect the sun here all day," George said. "A couple more of these, and this will be the brightest spot in the city. No one will be able to look up here without shielding their eyes."

The procession in town had ended, and Daniel knew he had to get home. There was no surprise that his father hadn't realized he was gone. His mother would have flipped La Loma inside out by now, but she worked the swing shift as a nurse's aide at Central Receiving Hospital downtown. Daniel suspected a young woman—perhaps one of the Herrera sisters—might be sitting on the front porch, counting how many push-ups the Champ could do. She'd eventually crawl up onto his back and dare him to do ten more, and when the Champ pretended he couldn't press up another inch, he'd roll over onto his side and she'd tumble on top of him and they both would laugh, and he would say *you smell like the ocean*, and she would swat his bare chest and say he'd better be careful because the ocean has a beautiful body that knows how to move, and he'd say *that's funny you should mention that, muñeca.* It was the Castillo family broken record.

"Do you remember your father?" asked Daniel.

"Barely," said George. "That was back in Iowa, a long time ago. My mother says he was a decent man, though."

Daniel winked. "You mean Krypton-Iowa."

"Daniel, I'm just a man like you'll be when you grow up," George said. "There's not a shred of difference between us."

This excited Daniel. "I knew it!"

Carlos and two men Daniel recognized from the railyard shined a red-and-white Coca-Cola flashlight in Daniel's face. "You knew what, Danny, huh? You think you're funny taking off like that?" said Carlos. He shifted the flashlight to Superman, who held his hands up to his face.

"If you don't mind, Mr. Castillo, I can explain," said George.

"Dios mio! You again, George Reeves. I must be the luckiest man in all Chavez Ravine to run into a television star two times in one day. Look who it is," he said to the two men who stood mostly unimpressed. "It's the Superman from that kids' show."

Superman pushed up from the ground with only one pants leg intact. He brushed the dirt from his hands and removed his necktie headband. "Look, I was just making sure Daniel was safe. I was concerned after I saw him run off," said George.

"I don't think that's your job." Carlos hit his chest with the flashlight. "I'm the jefe here, George Reeves. You are pretend."

"That may be," said George. He pointed to Daniel. "But that boy needs more than a jefe or a champ or whatever you want to call yourself."

Daniel traced the edge of the pocketknife on the outside of his pants. "It's my fault. I'm the one who ran—"

"I think maybe this is all a misunderstanding. I'll gather my things," said George.

Carlos walked around the Fortress of Solitude. "I see you cleaned up the dump."

"That's where I live now," said Daniel.

Carlos laughed and pushed Daniel to the ground. He poked Daniel's black eye with his finger. "You talk to me like that and maybe you need another one of these."

Daniel rolled out from underneath his father and crawled into the tunnel. Carlos and the two men kicked at the water heaters until Superman stepped between the three men. "That's quite enough, Carlos," he said. He put his hand on the tunnel wall and instructed Daniel to take the long way out and head home.

"I can see it in your eyes, George Reeves. I know that look better than anyone. I seen it in pendejos like you my whole boxing career. You're curious about my offer earlier today. Maybe you finally want to know what it's like to not hit in make believe, no?"

"What are you proposing?" asked George.

"Maybe you want a shot at my title," said Carlos.

"What good would come of that? I'm just gonna see to it that Daniel gets home safely, then I'll leave."

Carlos again shined the light in Superman's face. "You can tell all your rich friends how you stood toe to toe with the Champion of La Loma. And where you're from, that's still got to be worth something."

"What do you get out of all this?" George asked.

"Well, George Reeves, I get to be the Mexican that beat up Superman."

All of Chavez Ravine came to the witness the greatest fight card in the history of La Loma boxing—Manos de la Roca vs. the Man of Steel. Stores opened in the late night and vendors who typically took their carts down to city center during the day rubbed the sleep from their eyes to sell conchas and popsicles. The women prepared pumpkin and raisin tamales. Los veteranos put on full uniforms in case someone from the *Times* came to take pictures. The ring was made from milk crates and utility rope with white-caulked lines.

Superman apologized to Daniel that the day had come to this. He thanked him for his hard work building the Fortress of Solitude, said it was better than his own and that it really had been such a long time since he'd felt truly at home anywhere until now.

The two men stood under the single streetlight in La Loma. A growing ball of moths fluttered overhead. Carlos took off his shirt. The muscles on his chest resembled a marble staircase. He danced around the ring, delivering high-speed jabs at the hollering crowd. Carlos called Superman to the center of the ring with his fists. One of the men from the railyard worked Carlos's corner and held up a pair of boxing gloves to both men. Carlos shook his head. "No los necessito. I want George Reeves to feel this."

When Superman took off his shirt, his white gut flipped out over his waistband. There was no definition in his arms and a slight inward cupping of his shoulders. A patch of hair was the only feature that split his chest into two equal parts. It had been Daniel's single most anticipated moment, for everyone in attendance to see the shield on Superman's chest. Carlos called to the vendor selling sweet bread to come into the ring to serve his most loyal customer. Daniel took a place in Superman's corner.

Superman stretched out his fingers and advanced on the Champ. Carlos delivered the first blow. A technically sound right cross that crumpled Superman to the dirt. The crowd cheered as Carlos raised his hands into the air and pretended to fly around the ring. Daniel sensed that this might be Superman's number-one rule playing itself out. He slapped on the ground for his hero to rise up and get back in the fight. Superman rubbed his jaw. "I can see why you were the champ," George said. A voice called out from the crowd: *Hey, Superman, 'member that episode when you fought the bear? Get to it, amigo!* Superman stood up and thanked the voice from the crowd. Carlos's next combination included a flurry of body shots. All the boxing memory in the Champ's body had obviously not run out, and he painted Superman into the corner, pushing him over a stack of bushel barrels. Carlos yelled for Superman to get up, to stop being so damned maricón on the one night he should try to make a name for himself. When Superman finally threw his first punch, he telegraphed it so much that Carlos needed to only stroll out of its way. The retaliation Carlos delivered on Superman was so severe that the crowd covered their eyes. Some turned away completely, then decided to leave altogether. They had never witnessed anything like it before in La Loma. The Champ sat on Superman and punched his face repeatedly. Daniel felt in his own body, the pain attached to each blow. He begged for his father to stop, that he'd do anything his father wanted, that he'd become anything his father wanted him to be.

Superman turned his head toward the boy. Daniel noticed something that no one else had, something that no one in the world could have imagined happening except for him. Beneath the swelling in Superman's face, under the blood that began to clot and cake, was a man in such uncontrollable laughter that you'd swear he was a tickled child. Rule number two, Daniel thought. He pointed it out to the crowd, and stopped others from leaving. And the louder Superman laughed, the more frustrated Carlos became. He rained his fists down on Superman for what seemed like close to an hour. The blood splatter painted Carlos as his body weakened. When Superman did his best to catch his breath, he only did so that he might laugh from some place deeper inside his belly. Carlos finally collapsed off Superman onto his back. The crowd cheered for Superman. They chanted, *Hombre de Acero, Hombre de Acero!* Daniel wiped his father's body as he shivered with exhaustion and dehydration. The two men from the railyard dragged him from the ring and took him home.

Superman's whitewall tires had been stabbed with ice picks. The candy-cane boat of a car sat flat on the ground. Superman pulled off its hubcaps. "Take these, Daniel," said George. "You know what to do."

He limped into Genaro's Market and asked to use the phone. Alberto Cruz had worked at the store for close to a decade and knew Daniel well. He opened two sodas with a flathead screwdriver and placed them on the counter next to the phone. He shook Superman's hand. "Anything for the new champ," Alberto said. "And, champ, you talk as long as you want."

"I'm sure Mr. Cruz knows someone who can fix your car," said Daniel.

Mr. Cruz scrambled for the phone book.

"It's late. I'll get a tow truck coming," George said. "She'll be as good as new tomorrow."

They sat on the front step of Genaro's and waited for Superman's ride to arrive. The Man of Steel held a rubber water bottle filled with crushed ice to the left side of his face where the swelling had started to close his eye shut. Daniel made two trips inside the store to change out the ice. Mr. Cruz sent him out with a hot towel to drape around Superman's neck. Two young boys wrestled in the middle of the street. They grappled each other into headlocks and broke the straps on their overalls. Daniel threw chunks of ice and yelled for them to stop. Superman closed his good eye as Daniel slipped his glasses back onto his swollen face. "That's where those went," George said. "I'm not worth a damn without them."

Two sets of headlights bobbed up Bishop's Road. A flatbed tow truck and a black town car with darkened windows pulled up to the storefront. Superman waved. The tow truck mechanic stepped out and seemed surprised that it was George Reeves needing a tow. "Aren't you the TV Superman?" the mechanic asked. "It's hard to tell with your face. . . . Mister, are you okay?"

Superman handed the mechanic his keys. "Never better," George said. "They say I'm the Man of Steel."

"Do they now," said the mechanic.

Mr. Cruz came out of the store with his push broom to hit the boys still locked up and pretending to be the new champ. No one got out of the black town car. Superman only nodded to the barely visible driver through its darkened window. The mechanic attached a chain to the Chevy's underbelly and pulled it up onto the flatbed. He walked to the back of the car and attached a set of magnetic lights to the trunk. Heavy black wiring slapped each rear quarter panel.

"Be careful with her," Daniel chided. "She's one of a kind."

Superman whispered through his bloodied, bulbous lip. "That's right, son. You tell him."

Daniel helped Superman to his feet. Mr. Cruz muscled under Superman's right shoulder to give him support. A small gathering of Chavez Ravine residents gathered nearby, no doubt hoping to get one last look at the new welterweight champion. The children asked for autographs. Superman promised them he'd be back to sign every one when his vision improved. The women formed a circle around the black car. They draped Superman in orchids and yellow plumeria, oleander and Stargazer lilies. They prayed for Superman and signed the cross over his alien heart. Superman opened the back door and thanked Mr. Cruz for his kindness. He leaned on Daniel to balance himself as he let his body fall onto the backseat.

"We're birds, you and me," Daniel said. "Old crows."

Superman forced open his swollen eye. "The last two sons of Krypton."

Daniel shut the door and stepped away from the car. The neighborhood waved their good-byes as the car pulled away from the market steps. Mr. Cruz said he would never forget the day that actor George Reeves came to Chavez Ravine and left as the Last Champion of La Loma, that it would be as memorable to him as the day he opened his store for the first time. Everyone agreed and began their walk home.

The car stopped and the back door opened. Superman searched the hills for the Fortress of Solitude in the pitch black. Daniel anticipated the morning sun. When Superman stepped out of the car in his red boots and waved, he sent a vibration across the earth's crust that knocked Daniel off his feet. The car continued down Bishop's Road, where it eventually turned onto the Pasadena Freeway, heading away toward Benedict Canyon. Superman finally split open his bloodied shirt to reveal the Kryptonian *S* set against a yellow prism traced in crimson across his chest, the finely dimpled armor of his impenetrable blue skin. Daniel floated in the brief delay in gravity as Superman raised one arm and took flight, pulling all the clouds over Chavez Ravine through a burning hole punctured into the night sky.

ACKNOWLEDGMENTS

The highest level of consciousness one can attain is to be in a constant state of gratitude. This is a science measured by the collisions in my own lifetime. Let's call it love, and it starts here: My blessed mother, Rosalia Fierro Kaylor, despite the gravity in it all, you found our way through and brought me to the place where I could listen best to my heart and soul. Larry Kaylor, for your fatherly love and guidance. Nana, you painted on my heart the unconditional love, compassion, and faith of a thousand saints. Tata, my very best friend and superhero—you protected me in rocket ships and in the wash of transistor L.A. Dodgers games. My hand will forever be in the rough of yours. Nani, your love has always been an anchor in place and home. To family lost and now found. Shiloh, my heart is complete.

My thanks to Kathryn Conrad and the University of Arizona Press for inclusion in this honored Camino del Sol series. My heartfelt thanks to Kristen Buckles, Amanda Krause, Leigh McDonald, and Rosemary Brandt for the pure magic you poured over this work. To Pacific University MFA program director and friend Shelley Washburn for your kindness and devotion as I took the long walk into the wastelands. Tayari Jones, you invested in me when you didn't have to. Christine Sneed, for your sensibility and story heart, for being my hero at the eleventh hour. Colleen Sump, a mile above and a mile beyond. A very special thanks to *Poets & Writers Magazine*, Bonnie Marcus and Cathy Linh Che, Ann Napolitano, and the Maureen Egen Writers Exchange Award, for all your giving support. Manuel Muñoz and Helena María Viramontes, for your time and the lessons in your own work. Lorian Hemingway, for your encouraging words and generosity. Thank you, Neltje, Lynn Reeves, and the entire Jentel Artist Residency for the invaluable gift of stopping time and the Wyoming expanse. Kathryn Kulis-

Fierro, for showing me the value of the journey well traveled. David Ballenger, for your friendship and Spartan approach to this craft adventure. Ron Spatz at *Alaska Quarterly Review*, for your belief and lessons on fearlessness. Don Rearden, for more than a decade of storytelling navigation, kitchen genesis, and all the piñatas on all the streets.

Luis Alberto Urrea, you are the firing pin in this grenade. The engine inside your heart transforms pain into laughter and prayers. I am forever grateful for our warrior friendship. Jake Adam York, if I've ever written one *durable* and *lasting* word, it came from you. There's nothing in this craft if not for your lyric and the quest for the perfect BBQ. Jody Ellis, your steadfast and patient love saves me from daily capsize. All my love to you.

A special thanks to the Montebello Bat Cave, Newberry's, and Saint Jude's lair—for all the miraculous wonder and homemade tortillas a quarter mile off Atlantic Boulevard.

And finally to you, for following me home.

ABOUT THE AUTHOR

BRYAN ALLEN FIERRO holds an MFA from Pacific University in Oregon. He grew up in Los Angeles and now splits his time between L.A. and Anchorage, Alaska, where he works as a firefighter and paramedic. Fierro is the recipient of the *Poets & Writers* Maureen Egen Writers Exchange Award in Fiction.